Runaway Bride Violet

Cheryl Wright

Runaway Bride Violet

Dedication

To Margaret Tanner, my very dear friend and fellow author, for her enduring encouragement and friendship.

To Alan, my husband of over forty-eight years, who has been a relentless supporter of my writing and dreams for many years.

To You, my wonderful readers, who encourage me to continue writing these stories. It is such a joy knowing so many of you enjoy reading my stories as much as I love writing them for you.

Table of Contents

Chapter One

Rusty Hollow, Montana – 1880's

Violet Southerby took several fortifying breaths. She wasn't certain she could go through with this, or even that she should.

Just because her brother told Violet she had to, did not mean she should marry Brandon.

"Hurry, Violet. We must leave soon." Her mother's shrill voice coming through the bedroom door had Violet even more on edge. Nonetheless, she pulled her veil into place and added some additional hairpins to ensure it stayed in place.

Suddenly, the door was thrown open. "Honestly Violet. It's time to leave." Her mother glanced around the room. "For goodness' sake, you don't even have your shoes on yet!"

Exasperation was obvious in her mother's voice. How she wished Father was still alive. If he was here now, he would be the voice of reason. He could have calmed her mother by now and taken charge of the situation. And he would have told Violet it was all right to be nervous. Most brides were on their wedding day.

She longed for the strong arms of her father to hold her and tell her everything would be fine. Instead, her mother was running around the room like a fowl with its head cut off. Instead, chaos prevailed, as was always the case when Mother was involved.

Of course, if Father was here, she wouldn't be standing here in a wedding gown that was not of her choosing, and being forced into a marriage she definitely didn't want.

"What is going on in here?" Violet sighed. Her eldest brother's voice did not help. He would take charge and ensure the wedding went ahead as planned. It was the last thing Violet needed. Or wanted. "You look beautiful, sis." He glanced across at their mother and shrugged. They should be used to her theatrical antics by now, but she simply got worse the older she became.

Violet stepped forward and straightened her brother's tie. If she had to do this, the least her brother could do was look respectable. "Mother," Andrew said firmly. "You are required downstairs. Please hurry." He grinned at Violet. They both had a reprieve, but if she knew their mother, it would only be momentary.

"Thank you," she mouthed, still annoyed at her brother. "I couldn't have taken much more."

Andrew grinned. It was far worse on his wedding day, but at least the bride wasn't distracted by her nonsense.

"You are very welcome," he said as he moved in to hug his only sister. "Don't be nervous. Brandon is a wonderful man, and will take care of you."

His words were little reassurance. Telling her he'd canceled the wedding would be more to her liking. At least Andrew would give her away in the absence of their father, and that was somewhat comforting.

Suddenly, mother was standing in the doorway. "The wedding carriages have arrived," she said, her voice getting higher with every word. Andrew, who faced Violet, rolled his eyes and grinned.

Violet lifted her skirts to leave, and her brother glanced down. "Are you forgetting something?" he asked calmly.

Violet followed his gaze to discover her stocking'd feet.

Sitting in the carriage, jammed tight up against her brother, Violet could not control her anxiety. She twisted her hands in her lap and straightened her skirt several times.

"For goodness' sakes, Violet," Andrew said impatiently. "You're getting married, not going to your death."

Violet grimaced. It may as well have been the latter, because it was how she felt. "I barely know Brandon," she ground out. "I haven't seen him for years, and that was back when we were teenagers." She let out a long sigh. *Why did she let Andrew talk her into this nonsense?* She knew full well how it had come about. Her brother had inherited everything after Father died – the family home, the business, and all her father's money and worldly goods.

That included having to take care of his mother for the rest of her life, and Violet, his spinster sister. Until she married, that was, and then it would be up to her husband. Andrew had been selecting suitable men almost from the moment their father passed. There were several who were decidedly unsuitable, and she had rejected every one of them. Her brother's anger had grown to a point he'd disregarded her opinion and decided for her. And now, here she was – on the way to a wedding she wanted no part of.

"He is a good man, and *will* take care of you." Andrew pierced her with his stare, daring his sister to refuse. Besides, it was too late to turn back. They were literally around the corner from the church. Why Brandon had insisted on a church wedding, albeit a small one, Violet did not know. It wasn't like theirs would be a love-filled marriage. Quite the opposite. Andrew called it a marriage of convenience, Violet called it a forced marriage. Except for the lack of firearms or a baby in her belly, it could easily be called a shotgun wedding.

Her brother had left her no alternative. If she didn't go through with the marriage…? Andrew said he would never turn her out onto the street. It's what he'd said, but the frustrated expression he wore had her wondering.

The memory of that day had her heart pounding. She closed her eyes against the thought and pondered her position. *What if she didn't marry Andrew's childhood friend? Would her brother allow Violet to stay in the family home?* He said he'd already placed it on the market, but she highly doubted it – nothing proved that be the case. She was jolted back to reality when the carriage came to a sudden halt as they arrived at the church.

Violet swallowed. Hard.

How could she be expected to marry a man she barely knew? Last time she'd met him, Brandon Honeywell was an unruly teenager with a scruffy beard. Andrew had invited him to dine with them, and all had been fine, until Brandon had tried to kiss her as they strolled through the garden later that evening. The memory had her heart pounding again.

"Violet!" Andrew's voice broke into her thoughts. These were memories she preferred not to recall. *With company, Brandon came across as the perfect gentlemen, but when they were alone?* He had been enamored with her and let his feelings know.

Of course, her brother, ever loyal to his friend, refused to believe a word of it. *Was it any wonder she was reluctant to marry him?*

"Coming, Brother," she said between clenched teeth. It was too late to do anything now – she had no choice but to go through with the wedding. She pulled the veil down over her face before alighting the carriage and straightened her gown the moment she set foot on the ground. It would never do to enter the church in a rumpled wedding gown.

Violet straightened her shoulders and clutched the small bouquet Andrew had presented to her before they left the house.

As they neared the church, she heard organ music. It was really happening, and she had absolutely no choice in the matter. "Andrew… I," *Would he allow her to back out now?* She was promised to a man she barely knew. According to her brother, he was a pillar of society. Not here in town, but in the next county. *Was it convenient that he lived elsewhere and Violet knew little about him as an adult?*

The church doors opened for them, and Andrew hooked her arm through his. "Everything will be all right," he promised as he patted her hand. Violet gazed at him through the lace of her veil. *Would it?* She wanted to ask it of him, to demand it even, but the smile on his face told her to refrain. Violet had a feeling of foreboding in her stomach, and it wouldn't go away.

She suddenly pulled away and hurried outside. She heard a scuffle behind her. "Violet?" her brother asked gently. "What's wrong?"

She took several deep breaths before turning to face him. "I… I'm not sure I can go through with this." She glared at him now, aware this was completely his doing. Andrew had arranged the whole thing, totally without her permission or input.

He chuckled then. "Of course you can. All brides have second thoughts. It's normal, and called wedding day nerves." He wrapped his arm around her shoulder and led her back into the church. Andrew linked her arm with his and stepped forward.

She heard the collective sighs as she waited, alerting her to the fact their few guests, her mother and two witnesses, had noticed her leave. Violet felt the heat rise up her face and brushed at her cheeks as though that would fix her embarrassment. "Ready?" Andrew whispered, then, without waiting for an answer, guided her down the aisle past the small group of people sitting at the front. She had never seen the church so empty. It was curious to Violet. An upper class family like the Southerby's would normally be celebrating their only daughter's wedding. Instead her marriage was being hidden as though it didn't exist. It made absolutely no sense.

Her groom turned to face her as they got closer. Violet stared into his face – she didn't even recognize him. Brandon had changed so much since their last meeting. He had been handsome back then, but now, he almost took her breath away. Two men stood to the right of him, and if she didn't know better, she would think they were bodyguards. One thing Violet did know was she had no bridesmaids. She was forced into this wedding last minute, being told only yesterday, and had no opportunity to arrange anyone. Besides, her wedding was being kept secret. Once again, it confused her.

Brandon was clean-shaven, and his hair cut short. She recalled how unkempt he had been the last time she saw him, albeit years ago. There was no excuse – he could have, and certainly should have, cleaned himself up before visiting that day, even with Andrew being an old friend and a close one at that.

He reached out a hand, and Violet noticed his hands were soft and uncalloused. Whatever his work, Brandon didn't do hard labor. Given she'd been told his family was almost as wealthy as her own, she shouldn't be surprised.

"Violet," he whispered. "It is so good to see you again." His eyes seemed to twinkle, and they looked her over, but it was all Violet could do not to shiver against his scrutiny. She stood there glaring at this man who must surely know she didn't want to marry him, but he seemed totally unaffected. When she didn't take his hand, he lifted his fingers to her chin and faced her toward him. "Don't worry, we'll get to know each other again," he whispered. Whether he meant it or not, his words seemed to have an implication she didn't want to hear.

She had never known him, not really. And the last thing Violet wanted was to get to know this near stranger who wanted her for a wife. He leaned in then, and gently kissed her lips. It infuriated Violet. She was not yet his wife, and already he was taking liberties. She pulled back, and he didn't stop her, only snickered. *Or did she imagine that?*

She turned and faced her brother, and Andrew grinned. *Did he think this whole scenario was a laughing matter?* Violet certainly didn't. She stepped back, and her groom's arms came up around her. Brandon pulled her next to him, and the preacher cleared his throat, nodded at Brandon, then began the ceremony.

"I now pronounce you husband and wife," he said a short time later. "Congratulations Mr. and Mrs. Honeywell." Violet's head was spinning. *Did she really just marry an almost complete stranger?* Not that she was given any choice – everything had been arranged without her knowledge and she was the last to know. Even her mother, who couldn't keep a secret, knew about the wedding before Violet did.

She was in an impossible situation.

"You may now kiss your bride," the preacher continued.

Brandon grinned, then pulled her to face him, staring into her eyes as if assessing whether she would let him kiss her. Suddenly, making a decision, he leaned in and kissed her. Not chaste like the earlier kiss, but this was deep and emotional. His arm came up around her, and he pulled her closer, not giving Violet the opportunity to pull away.

That was when she felt it. There was a gun sitting against his chest. She heard her own intake of breath. As if the situation wasn't bad enough already, her legal husband was a pistol wielding man. *Why did he feel the need to do that? And at their wedding, no less.* Several scenarios went through her mind. *Was he a sheriff, a marshal, or a lawman of some sort? But the reality kicked in and realization hit her – had that been the case, her brother would have told her, wouldn't he?* No, her husband had to be an outlaw of some sort. Perhaps even wanted by the law.

The reason for the secret wedding suddenly came to light.

Before she could convince herself otherwise, Violet turned and ran out of the church without looking back. “Violet!” Andrew’s voice echoed through her mind as she jumped into the carriage intended to take the pair on their honeymoon.

Chapter Two

Carruthers sat up front, his back straight as always. "Where do you wish to go, Miss Southerby?"

It was a good question, and one Violet didn't know the answer to. "I… I'm really not certain," she answered, her voice as shaky as the rest of her.

"Violet!" Her brother's voice trailed behind her as they left the churchyard.

"Please hurry," she said urgently.

Carruthers had been with her family for many years and was as loyal as they came. "Would you like me to take you home, Miss Southerby?"

It was exactly where Violet wanted to go. She would climb the stairs to her room and remove the cumbersome wedding gown she never wanted to wear. She would let her hair down and brush it out, then happily crawl beneath the covers. But Violet knew home was the last place she should go.

It was bound to be the first place Andrew would look for her.

Not once did Carruthers ask what had happened or why her husband wasn't in the carriage with her.

Her mind was spinning with possibilities, and Violet couldn't think straight. "I have no idea," she answered as she brushed away tears as they streamed down her face. She pulled a lace handkerchief from her reticule and wiped them away before Carruthers noticed them. She glanced up to discover they had arrived at the train station.

They came to a halt and Carruthers turned in his seat and glanced back at her. "We have arrived at the station, Miss Southerby." He startled then, and Violet decided he realized she was no longer Violet Southerby, but now went by her husband's name. "Do you wish to travel by train, or should I take you elsewhere?"

What to do? Her mind was in disarray. Violet opened her reticule to place her handkerchief back inside it, and discovered a large wad of notes. *Had her mother added them?* It was the only explanation that made sense. There was no reason her brother would do such a thing, but neither would her mother. Agatha Southerby might put on airs, but she loved her daughter and had always looked out for her. She'd even tried to talk Andrew out of this ridiculous wedding, to no avail. Still, it was out of character for Mother. "What do *you* think, Carruthers? I'm rather confused."

He stared at her momentarily. "What I think, Mrs. Honeywell" he said, now using her married name, "is that I should take you to the next town. You can board the train there. Your brother is less likely to check there." With that, he nodded, his opinion affirmed.

"That," Violet said firmly, "sounds like an excellent plan." It was only moments later, and they were heading toward Cannondale – a town she hadn't visited for many years.

Violet sat down in the luxurious seat of the Pullman Coach. Her family was well known in the area, and all she had to do was make the request for a ticket – nothing else was required. Of course she was recognized the moment she stepped onto the train station, and the conductor was all over it.

"Of course we have space for you, Miss Southerby." He glanced about. "Where is your trunk?"

She held the carpetbag tightly. "I'm traveling lightly. This was a last-minute trip, and I doubt I'll be away long." Violet had no idea how long she would be gone. If she'd been thinking properly, which she wasn't since she was panicking, she would have asked Carruthers to unload the trunk the servants had packed for her honeymoon.

"Of course, Miss Southerby," he said. "Follow me." It wasn't long before Violet was seated and served a pot of tea with a small plate of cookies. As she glanced about, no other passengers had been afforded that privilege, and she wondered if she'd appeared distressed. Of course, no one else wore a wedding dress, and it wasn't until that moment Violet realized she still wore hers, complete with veil. She snatched the offending veil off her head and shoved it in the carpetbag. She had a change of clothes with her, as the plan, according to Andrew, was an overnight stay in a hotel before they headed to their destination.

She finished her tea and leaned back in the seat. It was far more comfortable than the sitting room chairs at home. And that was saying something. Always the best for the Southerby family, and nothing less. Violet breathed a sigh of relief. She had got here without incident, but would not be fully convinced until the train left the station.

A small group of older women boarded the carriage. They chatted between themselves and one woman nodded a greeting in her direction. Jonathan Campbell, their conductor, showed the women to their allocated seats. The same woman who greeted her, glanced curiously at her. It was then Violet was convinced she needed to change out of her wedding gown.

One thing she could be sure of, and that was Carruthers would never give her away. He was as loyal as they came, and had covered for her over the years, saving her from many a scolding from her parents.

"We will be traveling in a matter of minutes," Jonathan told her. "It's none of my business, but if you intend to be discreet, perhaps a change of clothing?" He began to walk away, then turned back. "I suggest you wait until after we've left the station. You don't want to be jolted to the floor."

It was good advice, and certainly advice she would take. Already it was apparent she was drawing attention. That was the last thing she wanted. If her new husband was a criminal, and Violet was certain he was, she didn't want him on her trail. Dressed as a bride, she was blatantly obvious, and all he had to do was ask if anyone had seen a woman dressed as a bride and they'd point in her direction.

Violet's heart thudded. How could Andrew put her in this position? Did he do it for the sake of the money he'd make from the sale of the family home? If that was even a motivation. It didn't make sense. If he wanted her out of the house, he could have asked. She would have been willing to move to somewhere far smaller. Her father had always provided a generous allowance, and she certainly wouldn't have been living in poverty. With only Violet and their mother living at home, along with a handful of servants, it had been clear for some time they had outgrown the family mansion.

None of it made sense, and it had Violet scratching her head.

The train whistle blew, alerting passengers to the fact they were about to leave the station. She stared out the window. No sign of Andrew or Brandon. So far, so good. Violet hoped that meant she had a clean getaway and would not have to worry about being pursued by her new husband, the criminal.

She sat patiently for the next few minutes, and then Jonathan was once again by her side. "You should be safe to change now. Let me accompany you to your sleeping quarters. You can change there and leave your carpetbag there until tonight if you wish." Violet followed him. It had been a while since she'd traveled by train. Last time she did, Father was still alive. The three of them went to Helena and had a combined holiday and shopping spree. Father was buying for business, but Violet and Mother were clothes shopping. Not that either of them really needed clothes – Father had brought them along for the ride. It was a pleasant change from their normal routine.

Violet regretted not having spent as much time with her father as she could have. Little did anyone know he would become ill and die within a matter of days. After his death, it was discovered he knew he was dying, and set up his will accordingly. Had she known, she would have asked for her freedom. Allowing Andrew to run her life until her marriage was not conducive to her happiness.

"Is everything all right, Miss Southerby?" Jonathan called through the door. Violet had not informed him she had actually married, nor that she'd intended to have the marriage annulled the first chance she got. She would ask the family lawyer to arrange the process. But for now, she had no choice but to accept she was now married and could be for quite some time.

"I'll be out shortly," she called back. Not having any input into her wedding gown didn't help. There were dozens of tiny buttons all the way down her back, and she was struggling. It made sense when she thought about it – Brandon would have planned it that way to ensure he needed to help her undress on their wedding night.

Violet sighed. The thought was repugnant to her.

"I could get one of the ladies to help, if you wish," he said, his voice a little lower this time.

She thought for a moment. Since she couldn't undo the buttons herself, she was left with little choice. "That would be splendid. Thank you," she called back. The silence told her he'd left to employ some help.

Violet sat on the side of the bed, fighting back tears. *How did it come to this?* At her age, it was always going to be more difficult to land a husband, but it wasn't something that bothered her. Violet had never been interested in marriage and had told her parents long ago. Andrew was completely aware of her position. Unfortunately, he'd taken it upon himself to marry her off and get her off his hands, anyway.

"Miss Southerby? I have Mrs. Hartford with me. She's going to assist you." Jonathan's voice was loud enough for Violet to hear, but not loud enough the entire carriage of passengers would get wind of it. They were far enough away from the day area for that.

"Of course, come in, Mrs. Hartford," Violet called back, and cracked the door to allow the other woman to enter. She smiled briefly as her savior entered the room, then closed the door quickly. "Thank you so much for your help," Violet told her new friend. "I have a slight dilemma; I can't reach to undo my gown."

"Don't mention it. Turn around and let me help." In no time, Violet felt the tension across her back loosen. "There you are, my dear. Is there anything else I can do to help?"

Why, she didn't know, but the mere presence of this woman, who was far older than Violet, had her feeling as though a weight had suddenly been lifted from her shoulders. "I think that's all, thank you. May I pay for your time?" Violet asked.

The look on the woman's face was one of disgust. "You most certainly can not!" she protested. "It was very obvious the moment I set eyes on you that you were in trouble." Her face softened then. "Do you want to talk about it?" She hastened to add only if Violet felt so inclined.

Violet straightened her shoulders and stared straight ahead. "I was married today," she said, her voice slightly above a whisper. "My brother forced me into it. My husband wore a gun." She glanced at the other woman to gauge her response.

"My goodness! That is totally unacceptable," she said, the alarm clear in her voice. "You ran?"

"I did," Violet said, as she twisted a handkerchief in her hands. "I was frightened and didn't know what else to do."

"The first thing you should do is change into whatever you have in that carpetbag." She helped Violet pull out her change of clothes and shoes, and carefully folded the wedding gown and placed it in the bag along with the expensive shoes that were purchased for her wedding. "Next, you must come and sit with my friends and I. You'll feel better being amongst other women who understand how troublesome men can be." She smiled then, and Violet felt better than she had since she'd discovered Andrew's plans for her marriage.

She stored her carpetbag where Jonathan had showed her and followed her new friend back into the Pullman Car. It didn't take long for Violet to feel part of the friendly group of women. They made her feel so comfortable, it was as if she'd known them for years.

Chapter Three

Violet awoke to the conductor directing passengers to awake. The train would stop at the next station in a little under two hours. Jonathan named the station, but in her slumbrous state, couldn't recall where that was. She still did not know where she would end up, but needed to make some sort of plan.

She'd had a restless night, and Brandon's face taunted her throughout the night. No matter how good looking he was, the fact he wore a gun to their wedding was something she would never forgive. Nor would she absolve her brother for his part in the contemptuous situation.

Violet glanced down as she sat on the side of the bed. She couldn't bring herself to wear the flimsy nightgown intended for her wedding night, and instead spent the night in her underwear. It was the best she could do.

She quickly dressed, albeit in the clothes she'd worn the day before, and headed out to meet with the other ladies for breakfast.

Mrs. Hartford and her friends had arranged for Violet to spend all her time on the train with them.

They'd all become great friends despite the short time they'd known each other. Now she couldn't imagine traveling without them, especially given her difficult circumstances. They were all long married and were all empathetic about Violet's situation. *How dare her brother put her in such a situation?*

It wasn't as though he needed the money. Their father had left Andrew in a very envious position for someone of his age. Had he been another twenty years older, he would still be the envy of Rusty Hollow, and indeed the entire county.

Instead of using his position for good, her brother had wielded his power over his younger sister to rid himself of her. The thought had Violet on the verge of tears. Noticing her new friends in the near distance, she straightened her shoulders and braced herself for the journey ahead. She clutched her reticule tighter, knowing the wads of money inside it were all she had for whatever time she had ahead of her – that might be days, or it may be months. Violet had no inkling at this point.

"Violet, my dear. Good morning to you," Mrs. Hartford said. The smile on her face quickly died. "You look exhausted my dear. You didn't sleep well?"

Violet glanced down at the expensive carpet on the floor of the Pullman Car. "Not at all, I'm afraid," she whispered. "My wicked husband's face crept into my dreams more than once."

"He's good looking, then?" one of the other women snickered, but Violet knew she was joking.

"Unfortunately, he is. But that doesn't mean I should have been forced to marry him." She sat herself down then and sank into the luxurious chair. She let out the longest sigh, as though that chair would change her entire life. Right now, that's exactly what it felt like.

"Breakfast is served," Jonathan announced moments later. "Please move into the dining car when you are ready." He was gone as quickly as he'd arrived.

"Shall we?" Mrs. Hartford asked as she stood. "I don't know about the rest of you, but I'm famished." Then she laughed, and Violet couldn't help but join her. It was the first time she'd laughed in what felt like forever. "You should laugh more often, my dear. Your smile becomes you," her new friend said. Violet knew she was right, her father had told her often.

How she missed Father. This ridiculous situation with Brandon would never have happened had Father still been alive. He would not have allowed it and may even have disinherited Andrew as a result. Instead of being punished for his awful deeds, Andrew had ended up with all the treasure their father possessed. It was blatantly unfair.

She shook herself mentally. It might be unreasonable, but there was nothing Violet could do about it. She knew years ago she would not inherit. Her mind focused for a moment. There was something in the back of her mind about her father's will, but try as she might, she couldn't recall what it was. No matter, it would come to her. Eventually.

"Miss Southerby?" The waitress stood at the end of the table with her order book, waiting patiently for Violet to answer. She'd been completely immersed in her thoughts and had missed the conversation entirely. "What would you like for breakfast?" she said, apparently repeating what she'd already said.

Violet stared blankly at the young woman. "She'll have what the rest of us are having – a full cooked breakfast." The waitress wrote down the order and walked away.

"I can't eat all that," Violet protested, despite the rumbling of her stomach.

"Phooey," Mrs. Hartford said. "You barely ate enough to feed a sparrow last night. Who knows what you will face today. Your best defense is to eat a hearty breakfast and keep your strength up." She reached for the freshly squeezed juice already delivered to each passenger.

Mrs. Hartford was right. Violet could not predict what she would encounter today. She hoped neither Andrew nor her new husband would locate her. *Was that even possible?*

"Violet?" Mrs. Hartford's voice cut into her reflections. "Do you have money to get you through? An allowance of some sort you can tap into?" Her friend appeared concerned. "If you need it, I'm willing to help."

"Thank you, but I have cash, secretly placed in my reticule. presumably by my mother. Now you mention it, I do have an allowance. I rarely spend money and had forgotten about it. I charge most of my expenses to the family account." Father's will – that's what she was trying to recall. Her allowance was to continue, even after she married. It meant she could withdraw money as she required it. There would already be a decent sum waiting for her, and it would allow her to settle wherever she wished. It was an immense weight off her shoulders.

Breakfast arrived, and the group spent the next half an hour eating and discussing their plans for the next few days. Violet was invited to join them on a shopping trip when they arrived at Aurora Ridge in a few days time, and was sorely tempted. At the moment, she was taking one day at a time. They understood, but hoped she would reconsider. She was desperate for clothes, so most likely would. The thought had her smiling.

The days passed in a flash. Violet couldn't believe she'd slipped through her brother's net, and therefore enjoyed the days with her newfound friends. The train was scheduled for a five hour stop which allowed the group spend the day at Aurora Ridge replenishing her wardrobe. Instead of depleting the cash she'd found in her reticule, she visited the bank and withdrew a tidy sum to pay for her purchases. Violet was relieved she now had clean clothes to wear. Mrs. Hartford was around Violet's size, and had lent her two blouses to see her through. Violet was far more grateful than she could ever put into words.

As she stood in front of the cashier waiting for her change, a feeling of foreboding came over her. Violet shuddered as she accepted her purchases from the cashier who had no doubt made a huge commission on the shopping spree of Violet and her new friends.

A hand landed gently on her shoulder and Violet was startled. "Are you all right, Violet?" Mrs. Hartford's kind voice helped calm her shattered nerves.

She nodded. "It felt like I was being watched," she said, then shook her head. "That's crazy, of course.

No one knows where I am, except for you ladies. And Jonathan, but he wouldn't divulge my whereabouts." She gazed at the older woman. "Would he?"

"Absolutely not! Come on, it's time to return to the train." Violet was pleased with her new clothes, and warmth filled her. For the first time in days, she felt happy. Since she'd run out on her wedding, Violet had been filled with dread. Now, because of the new friends she'd made, she was certain everything would be all right.

She clutched her reticule tightly, knowing exactly what was inside, and gripped the handles of her shopping bag to ensure she didn't drop it. Or worse, someone stole it. "I really enjoyed lunch today," she told the women surrounding her. "I do hope we can keep in touch after this is all resolved."

"I certainly hope so," Mrs. Hartford said. Mrs. Carrington and Mrs. Jefferson agreed. Soon they were all hugging, then continued on to their destination. By the time they returned, the group was ready for afternoon tea.

"It's too early to board the train," their conductor said. "The staff are still cleaning the car, but it shouldn't be much longer. Apologies for the delay." He looked genuinely sorry, and Violet felt for him.

Around ten minutes later, he ushered the group onto the train. "Did you enjoy your shopping, Miss

Southerby?" Jonathan asked as the rest of the group walked ahead and into the Pullman Car.

"Indeed I did," she answered, but again had that feeling of foreboding. Violet glanced to her left, then to her right. All was clear. She laughed then, feeling rather foolish.

"I'm truly sorry, Miss Southerby," Jonathan said, then stepped aside. Before she could grasp what was happening, Violet was gripped by the arms and dragged back onto the street. Andrew! It had to be her brother. She couldn't blame Jonathan. After all, Andrew was a force to be reckoned with.

She tried to scream, but before she could make a sound, a strong hand clasped tightly around her mouth. When Violet managed to glance at her attacker, she was shocked to find it wasn't her brother after all, but Brandon Honeywell who dragged her away from her friends, and from safety. "I'm sorry," he said gruffly, then continued to pull her out of the station.

The moment they were on the street, a carriage arrived, and Brandon shoved her inside. Violet was unsure of her future. *Was she about to become a slave to this man, or did he intend to kill her?* Neither thought was palatable, but he'd captured her, and she was unable to escape.

"How dare you!" she screamed as the carriage pulled away.

Brandon faced her, then stared, his lips tightly pursed. Then leaned back against the seat and laughed. "You always were a feisty one," he said, still chuckling.

"I don't appreciate being man-handled by you or anyone," Violet spat at him. "Just because you're my husband doesn't give you the right…"

"According to Andrew, *and the law*, it does." He crossed his arms and grinned at her. Her first instinct was to slap his face, but Violet did not know what *this* Brandon Honeywell was capable of. The old Brandon would never have treated her this way.

Instead she sat quietly, hoping it was all a dream. "We have a distance to go," he whispered. "Can't stay too close to town."

Violet stared at him. First he was mocking her, then he was keeping her informed. Her head was spinning and she was totally confused. As she sat beside him, she noticed Brandon's gun was still beneath his jacket. It made her shudder, just as she had earlier when she was certain she was being watched. "Did Jonathan tell you where I was? Otherwise, I do not know how you found me." She glared at him then, and he tried to force back a smile.

"Not Jonathan. Andrew received an account for your travel. We checked the timetable and worked out where I could best catch up with you. Those spare hours at Aurora Ridge were extremely helpful." He grinned then, and again, she wanted to slap him.

"You always were infuriating," she spat, then turned sideways to ensure she didn't have to look at him.

She heard him chuckle again, then Brandon's hand crept up her back and onto her shoulder. A shiver went down her spine, and she knew it had to be because she found him so repugnant. But Violet realized it wasn't true. As a young man, she'd thought him the most handsome man she'd ever met. She'd even felt drawn to him. There was only reason she didn't allow him to kiss, and that was his unruly state. Had he been well-groomed, she more than likely would have allowed him take her in his arms and kiss her until she was breathless.

Teenage hormones, she supposed. But she was an adult now, and not the pathetic girl she was back then. Certainly not mindless enough to allow someone like Brandon to steal her heart, especially knowing the man was a hardened criminal. He might be even more handsome than she remembered, but that did not compensate for the ghastly deeds he had no doubt undertaken.

How could someone from Brandon's background turn into an outlaw? Andrew had to be aware of the man's criminal behavior. She refused to believe otherwise. The strange thing was, her brother hadn't mentioned Brandon for quite some time. Years, in fact. Not that Andrew spoke with her often. He had the worry of running Father's business. Well, it was Andrew's business now, and that really got her riled up. If she had been born male, the business would be hers. At least partially. It really wasn't fair.

She tried to shake off Brandon's advances by moving to the other side of the carriage, and felt his hand stiffen. Obviously not one to be easily put off, she felt his other hand snake up and around her waist. He gently pulled her back to lean against him. Violet felt herself being drawn to him as though she were that naive teenage girl all those years ago.

And then she felt the gun underneath his jacket.

She abruptly sat up, then turned to glare at him. "Must you carry that ghastly thing everywhere?"

"I do not know what you're talking about," Brandon said, confusion clear on his face.

"The pistol."

Suddenly, his expression cleared. "Is that why you ran? Because of this?" He opened his jacket slightly to show her the pistol that sat firmly in the holster. "It's for protection, nothing more." She didn't believe a word he said and scowled. "It's true, I promise." He pulled her to him again and gently kissed her neck. Violet heard herself groan and abruptly sat up. *What was it about Brandon Honeywell that had her acting this way?*

The carriage pulled to a halt, and Violet glanced about. "Where are we?" she asked. They must be well out of town, she decided, since there were no buildings in sight. It really bothered her. *Exactly how isolated were they?* It would make escape difficult.

"It's a little hideaway my family has owned for years. I think you'll like it." Their driver opened the carriage door, and Brandon alighted, then helped Violet down the steps. "I'm really not the monster you seem to believe I am," he said, a smile playing on his lips.

"Welcome to the Travelers Rest Hotel." An older woman stood in the doorway, a smile on her face. "I didn't think I'd ever see the day," she said as she flicked her apron. She then turned and went inside.

Violet smiled at the use of the word hotel. This far out of town, no one would build a hotel. *Or would they?*

"George and Martha Black," Brandon explained. "They've worked and lived here for as long as I can remember."

The *little hideaway,* as Brandon had called it, was smaller than her own family's mansion, but certainly not what you would call a hideaway. As she stepped inside, Violet couldn't believe what she was seeing. The building was the size of a small hotel and decorated similarly. "I thought you said it was a hideaway," she said accusingly. "It's nothing of the sort."

He shrugged, then led her to a room at the top of the stairs. "This is the honeymoon suite," her husband told her as he wiggled his eyebrows. His attitude was beginning to infuriate her.

Violet stared at the painted sign that confirmed his words. "So, it truly is a hotel?"

"It is, but this is the quiet time of the year, so we have it all to ourselves. George and Martha have their own accommodations at the back of the building."

Brandon opened the door and ushered her inside, placing her recently purchased bag of clothes on the floor. "What about my carpetbag? I guess that's gone forever." The latter was a statement, not a question, and she pouted at him, obviously still smarting from his heavy-handedness at the station.

"What was in it?" He stared at her, daring Violet to get sassy with him.

Still pouting, she replied. "My wedding dress and shoes, and my nightgown." She lifted her chin high, and Brandon knew he was in for the ride of his life with his new bride.

"Jonathan will store it until we can collect it. Not that you'll need the wedding dress again." He recalled the way she looked in that wedding gown. He'd fallen head over heels in love with her the first time he ever met Violet, but Andrew warned him off. For years, Brandon had played the field, never staying with one woman for long. Violet had spoiled him that way. He'd complied with Andrew's demand, but never forgot her.

He closed the door behind him, and removed his jacket, hanging it in the wardrobe. Violet stared at his chest. "Do you really need that thing?" she spat at him. "I despise guns."

He studied her momentarily. Not that he could tell Violet, but he needed to keep it close. One never knew when it would be needed.

"You're not sleeping in here," she added, her annoyance with him coming through loud and clear.

He smiled then, knowing his smile came across as wicked. He could feel it. His mood had changed. Whether that was because they stood in the honeymoon suite, he did not know. But that was exactly where they were. His beautiful wife stood within arm's length, and all he wanted to do now was wrap her in his arms and kiss her for the rest of his life. Unfortunately, he was fully aware of her stance. Violet hated him. Not only because they forced her to marry him, but because he'd snatched her from the train station. She seemed happy with her friends, and he was loath to remove her, but how else could he…

"Get out!" She faced him now, hands on hips and her face dripping with annoyance. "Find your own room." She glared at him, and Brandon realized he was about to face the wrath of Violet. The temper Andrew had warned him about.

Instead of leaving, instead of answering her, laughter bubbled up inside of him. Here was this petite woman standing in front of him, demanding he leave. He was nearly a foot taller than her, and far stronger, and yet… he found it laughable, but at the same time, it was endearing. "Violet," he said gently. "We are married. We missed our wedding night, and so tonight's the night." He grinned far more than he should have. Brandon knew he shouldn't play with her. All that would do was get her even more riled up.

He stepped toward her, and Violet took two steps back. His hands came up and gently gripped her arms, holding her in place. Without thinking, he pulled her close and wrapped Violet in his arms. He'd waited years for this moment.

When Andrew came to him less than a week ago, Brandon didn't know he would soon be married to his childhood sweetheart. Except she wasn't his sweetheart, not really. It was how he always thought of her, but Violet despised him. She always had. It was completely his fault for trying to kiss her that day. Andrew had warned him not to lay a hand on his sister and had kept Brandon away from her ever since.

It was the biggest mistake of his life.

But now they were married. Not that she was happy about it. He couldn't blame her. Andrew demanded she not be told the truth, and it was killing Brandon not to tell her. She deserved to know.

A flash of light outside had him hurrying to the window. He pulled the curtains closed and peeked behind them. In the semi-darkness he saw someone, a man, hurry toward the building. Now Brandon was on alert. He should have gone with his original plan, but Andrew wouldn't have it. *Marry my sister instead*, he said, killing two birds with one stone. Brandon was loath to do it, but knew it was the only way.

He was in two minds about the situation, knowing full well Violet hated him. Their kiss had lasted a matter of seconds, but it changed everything. From that day forward, according to Andrew, he was banned from the house when Violet was there, and which was most of the time.

"Sit over there and keep quiet," he told her firmly. Violet scowled at him. "Don't argue, just do it. And stay there, don't move until I say so." By now she was fuming. There was no doubt in his mind. Despite her anger, she did as she was told.

Brandon left the room, locking it behind himself. He heard the rattle of the doorknob as Violet attempted to open the locked door. He could only imagine how angry she was. But it was for her own safety.

He near ran down the stairs, pulling out his gun and headed toward the front door. It was the obvious place for them to enter, as it was the easiest point of entry. The door shook as whoever was out there tried to break in. Light showed under the door, proving he was right. It wasn't the wind causing the door to rattle.

Andrew knew the risks, and didn't listen. Now it was up to Brandon to ensure her safety. If he shot the fool, Violet would get suspicious. If he did nothing, she would still be in danger, and he couldn't allow that. Either way, he was certain more would follow. This one man wouldn't be the only one. He'd been a fool to bring her here. He'd deal with this now because he had to, but things had to change, otherwise his new wife wouldn't last until the morning.

Chapter Four

"What do you mean, there was an intruder?" There she was, again with her hands on her hips. She was feisty. He'd give her that. It was her father's fault; he'd let Violet have her way most of her life. And now she was Brandon's problem.

"I dealt with him. I tied him up and locked him in the downstairs closet. George Black, our carriage driver, will deliver him to the sheriff in the morning."

"Oh, well, that's all right then," she said in that sassy way that was growing on him. It was all Brandon could do not to grin.

"Now, where were we? Oh yes," he said flippantly as he stepped forward to wrap her in his arms again, but she pushed him away.

"Why did you lock me in here? I was petrified." Suddenly, her expression changed, and she looked like a frightened little girl. Brandon pulled her to him again and held her against his chest. He didn't care what Andrew thought; she needed to know. But not tonight. He'd have to find the right time to tell her, and that wasn't now. He had no idea when it would be, but he refused to worry her even more tonight.

At first Violet stood stiff as a board, but after his hands circled across her back, she sank into him. "I'm sorry, I truly am," he said. "I was trying to keep you safe." She nodded against him, and it was all he could do not take things further. What he wanted most of all was to kiss her. He promised her brother he wouldn't do that, and wouldn't treat her like she was his wife, even though she was. Every moment he spent with Violet was another moment that had him questioning why he'd made the promise. She was, after all, his teenage crush. Not that Andrew had allowed him to get near her back then.

The only reason he'd married her? Andrew was desperate.

"Brandon," she whispered. "I'm exhausted. And hungry." She glanced up at him with those big brown eyes and he felt himself melting. Andrew had given him an assignment, and it was up to Brandon to follow through.

His hand came up of its own accord and caressed her cheek. Violet didn't object, but he knew Andrew would.

"Of course you're hungry. It's late. I'm sure there's something in the kitchen we can cook. Any other time of the year, the inn is busy – often full to the rafters with guests. Right now, we're the only visitors and most of the staff are on a break, until the busy time starts again."

She studied him then. "This is your parent's business, right? I thought it would be busy all year round." He swallowed hard. She could see right through him, and Brandon was going to have to be careful, or she'd find out the truth despite what her brother wanted.

"It's quiet for a couple of weeks each year. The rest of the time is busy – it gives the staff a well-deserved break." He hated lying to her, but until he felt the time was right, he would keep Violet in the dark. He feared that time was not too far away.

She reached out and took his hand, taking Brandon by surprise. He stared at their entwined hands and winced. As much as he loved the feel of her hand in his, he couldn't get used to it. Once all this was over, their marriage would be annulled. Someone in his situation couldn't have a wife or family. It was far too dangerous – for them.

He sighed inwardly. He'd spent all these years yearning for a wife, knowing it was not an option. It was a decision he'd made long ago, and still stood by it. Violet's presence was forcing him to rethink, but despite that, he had to stand by his decision.

She pulled him toward the door, and they went downstairs together. With each step, he was forced to inhale her fragrance. Lavender, if he wasn't mistaken – his mother had a lavender bush in the garden she spent so much time in. He glanced across at her, and Violet turned to face him at that very moment.

Brandon opened his mouth to speak, then slapped it shut. The less he said the better. He didn't want to communicate with her and become attached. He was here to do a job, and by gosh, he would do it. After that, he would disappear into the night, never to be seen again. By Violet, at least.

Once they reached the kitchen, he lit the lantern that sat just inside the door. He stood back and watched as Violet opened cupboard after cupboard, trying to locate food. "There's a large pantry over there," he said, pointing in the right direction. "Wait until I bring the lantern over. I don't want you to fall." The skirt she wore seemed a little long, and it was certainly a possibility. Back home, she no doubt had a seamstress who would take care of such issues, but in Aurora Ridge it would have been strictly over the counter. He was certain that would have been a thing of contention. But if it was, Violet hadn't mentioned it.

Standing in the doorway to the pantry, he saw a shelf with bread, eggs, and flour, plus a few other staples. Violet reached down into the icebox and pulled out bacon and butter. "Bacon and eggs with toast it is then," she said as she chuckled. "The best wedding feast there ever was."

Without warning, she stared at him, then suddenly went quiet. *Was she thinking about what could have been if she hadn't run?* In a way, he was glad. He felt like a fraud as it was. If he'd had to go through a meal with their guests as well, he probably wouldn't have ever forgiven himself. He still carried the guilt from being part of Andrew's devious plans.

"Sounds good to me," he said, and took some items from her. She followed him out and placed all the produce on the kitchen counter. Violet seemed right at home in the kitchen, which surprised him. He knew for a fact the Southerby's had a cook. "The question is, can you put them together to make a meal?" He laughed then, not wanting her to think he was criticizing. He went straight to the stove and ensured it was burning well. It was fired up enough but wouldn't last the night. He'd be sure to add to it before they retired for the night.

He stood back and watched as Violet made the simple meal. He found a bottle of wine, but had second thoughts. He needed to keep his wits about him, and didn't want to risk getting his wife drunk. He did not know if she could handle alcohol or not, and she may need to be at her best. Instead, he made tea for Violet, and strong black coffee for himself.

He couldn't afford to fall asleep. Things might get tricky and he needed to be wide awake.

Brandon found cutlery and napkins, then set one table in the small dining room. He placed a lantern in the center of the table and returned to the kitchen.

"It's ready. I hope it's acceptable." She smiled at him then, a small coy smile, and it warmed his heart. He admonished himself for feeling that way. He'd promised Andrew. That thought brought him back to reality, and he took the plate she handed him.

He pulled out her chair, and pushed it in when she was settled, then sat opposite. "It's very romantic, don't you think?" She raised an eyebrow at him. Violet was behaving in the total opposite way to what he'd expected. When he'd snatched her earlier in the day, she was furious. *Now she was being seductive? What was going on?*

She reached for his hand and said a quick prayer of thanks for the meal, taking Brandon by surprise. His hackles were up. She was being more than compliant, and that was always suspicious to his way of thinking. "Eat up," she said, and smiled at him.

She had officially gone from being as mad and as wild as a mountain cat to a new bride who was smitten with her husband. Something didn't make sense. He would think about it, but for now, he'd eat his food.

Violet was tucked up in bed, waiting for her husband to join her. Only he didn't. Brandon settled himself on the comfortable chair in the corner and made no attempt to join her.

When they'd returned to the bedroom, he'd taken her in his arms, and it convinced Violet he would kiss her. He'd held her so close, his fingers caressing her cheek. She melted into him and never wanted him to let her go. It was then she remembered it was a ruse, that she was only pretending to let him think she'd changed her mind. Once he was asleep, she planned to sneak out of the room and out of the house. Then she would steal away into the night, never to be seen again.

At least not by Brandon or her devious brother, the rotter's.

Violet fumed when she thought about Andrew. He'd pretended to love her, to want the best for her, when all he really wanted to do was get rid of her, and make her someone else's problem. Why that someone had to be Brandon, she would never know. Out of all the men he knew, Andrew had to choose his childhood friend. As far as Violet was aware, the two hadn't even spoken for years.

Andrew had arranged many suitors, some of them were even close to acceptable – why didn't he choose one of them?

Violet shook her self mentally. Not one of the men Andrew had wanted her to marry were suitable. Mostly because they weren't her choice. She wanted to marry for love, not for any other reason. It was why her forced marriage went so much against the grain. Even her parents had married for love, which was virtually unheard of at the time. Especially with their families being so wealthy. The perfect match for each family was the accepted thing back then. And even now. Which was even more reason for her to be confused about Andrew's choice of the perfect match for her.

"Aren't you coming to bed, my love?" Violet asked, using the most seductive voice she could muster. He looked settled for the night, which was confusing.

"Soon," he said as he glanced about the room. Her heart thudded. For her plan to work, she needed Brandon to come to bed and eventually fall asleep. If that meant she had to endure him making love to her, then so be it.

"On second thoughts," she said, thoroughly annoyed he'd thwarted her plan, "I need to use the privy." He stood. "It's just down the hall. I can go alone," she ground out, utterly and totally frustrated by now.

"I'm coming with you," he said, brushing his hair back off his face.

Violet took a deep breath and silently counted to ten. *Why hadn't Mother told her how frustrating men could be?* She already knew Brandon could be a pain, which was the reason he'd irritated her so much when they were younger. He always had to get his own way, and he really hadn't changed.

She climbed out of bed and turned to face him. "I will be fine. The bathroom is mere steps away. It's not like someone is going to run off with me." Despite feeling so tense, she chuckled then, seeing the mirth in her own words. Except Brandon didn't laugh. Instead, his lips formed a tight line, and all color drained from his face. "Brandon? You're frightening me."

He stepped toward her and took her in his arms. "I don't know how to tell you this," he whispered, pulling her closer still.

She pulled away and stared up into his face. She could feel herself shaking. Violet had never been so scared in her life. "What has my brother done?"

Violet sat quietly, listening to everything Brandon had to say. Andrew was being blackmailed for the business. As the richest family in their county, the Southerby's had a lot to lose. But for Andrew, according to her husband, the most precious thing the criminals threatened was to kill Violet if they didn't get what they wanted.

She gasped at his words, and she felt the color drain from her face. Despite sitting down, she felt light-headed and was certain she would to faint. Only she wouldn't let that happen. Violet needed to keep her wits about her.

"The intruder? He was trying to…" she gulped. "kill me?" Tears formed in her eyes, but she fought them back. "Why didn't Andrew simply tell me?" Now she was angry. Her brother had a lot to answer for.

"He didn't want to scare you." His words were simple, but powerful. Andrew did love her, after all.

She swallowed down the emotion. "I thought…" she swallowed again, forcing herself not to cry. "I thought he wanted to rid himself of me." She bent her head and this time, the tears flowed. She'd finally said the words she believed were true.

Brandon reached over and took her hands in his own. "Get rid of you? Your brother loves you far more than you realize." He stood then, and pulled Violet to her feet, pulling her close, and wrapping his arms tightly around her.

"What's your part in all of this?" She had to ask, since it was the one thing Brandon hadn't vocalized.

"I'm your bodyguard." His words were succinct and brutal. She should have understood his position from the start. There was no love lost between them. That kiss all those years ago – she'd slapped his face and left an unsightly red mark. He'd left almost immediately, and Violet had never set eyes on him again.

Her fingers went to her lips, the memory still with her after all this time. "What do we do now?" Violet knew what she wanted to do, and that was to go to the authorities. Perhaps have them lock her up until they found the criminals.

Then it hit her. "Wait. I thought *you* were a criminal. The gun…" Now she really was confused, but instead of defending himself, Brandon laughed.

"No, Ma'am." He reached inside his jacket and pulled out a badge, cradling it in his large hand. "Marshal Brandon Honeywell at your service, Ma'am." He put the badge away again. "Most people call me Buck."

Her heart thudded. She'd heard of Marshal Buck Honeywell, but hadn't put two and two together. It was all making sense now. "And the marriage?"

"It was Andrew's way of keeping the truth from you. Besides, he knew your reputation would be ruined if we spent time alone without a chaperone, and that was never going to happen."

Her head was spinning, and Violet was emotionally drained. "I'm exhausted. It's a lot to take in." She pulled away and began the trudge up the stairs to their room. The Honeymoon Suite.

She climbed into the luxurious bed but knew she wouldn't sleep. Especially knowing people were out there trying to kill her. Murder her. *And for what? Money? Prestige?* She fought back a sob. "Come to bed," she said quietly when Brandon set himself up on the chair again.

"Your brother…" He appeared alarmed at her request.

"Forget Andrew. Come to bed." She patted the space beside her, and he stepped over to the enormous bed, and undressed. Violet swallowed as she watched him remove first his shirt and then his pants. The man certainly was good to look at.

He climbed into the bed and turned away from her.

"Am I that repulsive?" she asked, feeling totally rejected.

He cleared his throat. "I promised Andrew I wouldn't touch you," he whispered, his voice full of, she wasn't sure what. Regret?

"Forget Andrew," Violet whispered. "We're married, and I need you close to me."

Brandon turned to face her, and Violet leaned in and kissed him. Only this kiss wasn't as chaste as the one he stole when she was a teenager.

Chapter Five

Now the truth was out in the open, Brandon thought it should make things easier. Except last night changed everything.

He was still in love with Violet, had been since the day they met. Why he'd promised Andrew to keep his hands off her, Brandon would never know. The damage was done, and there wasn't a thing either he or Andrew could do about it.

As they alighted the stairs, he could hear Martha Black rattling about in the kitchen. At least he hoped it was her. When they got to the bottom, he pushed Violet behind him. "What is wrong with you?" she asked, her annoyance clear.

"Someone is in the kitchen."

She sighed then. "Don't you know the sounds of someone cooking? Honestly, men," she said, then reached for his hand.

He savored the feel of her soft hands. A shiver ran through him at her touch. He knew she was using him, the same way Andrew had used him, but Brandon had feelings for his wife, and always had. The worry, for him anyway, was after it was all over. When they caught the criminals, they would go their separate ways. Violet didn't love him. Last night was more about comforting her than anything else. For her, anyway. It certainly wasn't the way Brandon felt.

The thought of losing her cut through his heart. He'd spent years trying to forget her, but it had proven impossible. She was imbedded in his heart, his mind, his entire being, and wouldn't, for even a moment, leave him in peace. Instead of pining for her, he'd thrown himself into his work. He'd kept in touch with Andrew when he could, and kept tabs on Violet, but vowed never to see her again. It was the only way he could survive without her in his life.

And that's what he did – survive. Barely.

Thoughts of her affected his work, his life, but he promised himself to get over her. He never did. Andrew's request was a difficult one for Brandon, but he accepted. Only because he loved her so much and knew he had to keep Violet out of harm's way.

"Ah, it's the newlyweds," Mrs. Black said, smiling broadly. "It's so nice to finally see you settled, Brandon."

If only she knew the truth, Mrs. Black would be disgusted with him. He'd been brought up better than this. Violet wouldn't stay with him after this was all over. She would run back home, where she felt comfortable. One thing was certain; she would have a piece of her brother. He could already picture it – his wife, tiny as she was, would have her hands on her hips and would tear into him. The vision made him chuckle.

“What’s so funny?” Violet demanded, her eyes full of suspicion.

He stopped laughing then. “Nothing.”

“Brandon Honeywell, tell me the truth!” She pierced him with her eyes, and he squirmed under her scrutiny. He’d confronted offenders with firearms far bigger than Violet and not even flinched, but recoiled when she challenged him.

“I was thinking of the conversation between you and Andrew when I deliver you back home.” She stared at him. “After you’re safe again,” he added. She seemed disappointed, and it confused him.

Mrs. Black chose that very moment to put a plate of food in front of him, distracting him from the conversation. “You need to eat up, Mrs. Honeywell. You’re far too skinny.” She was gone before Violet had a chance to answer.

“I’m not skinny,” she told Brandon after the older woman was gone.

He shrugged then, not sure what to say, so instead changed the subject. “We need to leave here,” he said. “It’s very clear it isn’t safe for you here. I stupidly thought it would be.” He frowned then, and

Violet wondered what he was thinking. "We'll leave after breakfast."

"Where are we going?"

"Right now, I do not know. But it needs to be far from here."

Sitting next to Violet in the carriage, Brandon clutched her hand. They'd come so far in such a short time, but he was fully aware he was merely comforting her. There was no love lost between them, not now, and he knew there never would be. "We'll arrive at the station shortly," George Black told them. He'd taken them to another town, one that was out of the county, hoping to be more discreet.

Shady Glen was a far smaller station than Aurora Ridge, according to Old George, as Brandon called him. That meant they couldn't hide in plain sight. On the plus side, neither could her pursuers. Brandon glanced about, taking in every person, every doorway, and every potential place there was to hide. She clutched at his arm. "It's fine," he whispered. "It appears safe."

Violet breathed a massive sigh of relief. They have only a little luggage with them. Violet had her shopping bag with her new clothes, and Brandon has a small overnight bag. They are as subtle as possible, trying not to look like the newlyweds they are. "Have you worked out where we're going yet?" She appeared concerned, and Brandon couldn't blame her. He is every bit as worried as she is, if not more. Keeping her safe is paramount.

"We can use the Pullman Car when the train arrives. Only those of a certain standing in the community can afford to buy tickets." She smiled tentatively at him, and Brandon realized she thought they would be safe on the train.

"No Pullman Car." He stared down at her. "How do you think I found you?" He squeezed her hand then, trying to portray some reassurance. *But how did you reassure someone else when you weren't convinced yourself?*

It wasn't long before the train pulled into Shady Glen station. An apt name, Brandon decided. Soon after, a familiar figure appeared, then disappeared again. He strode up to them not long after, a bag in his hands, and his arms outstretched. "Ah, Mrs. Honeywell," Jonathan said. "Your carpetbag."

Brandon put a finger to his lips. "We are endeavoring to travel incognito. No names, please."

Jonathan appeared confused, but complied. "Of course. I'll arrange for two tickets in the Pullman…"

Brandon interrupted him. "Not this time. And please, don't alert anyone to our presence here." The other man seemed even more confused.

"I didn't last time. I promise, I didn't." He glanced at Violet.

"I know," she said. "You are a loyal friend. Thank you," she said, then leaned in and hugged him.

Brandon cleared his throat. "We should get off the platform. We're sitting ducks here."

Jonathan ushered them into one of the public carriages, clearly unhappy.

"Well, this is different," Violet said, a tentative smile on her face. The public carriage was a far cry from what she was used to. Brandon, on the other hand, didn't mind. He'd only used the Pullman Car when he was younger. He despised the way people were categorized by how much money they had.

He studied their surroundings. Their carriage was near to empty, which he preferred. It meant fewer people for him to monitor. "We'll sit here." He indicated two seats close to the door, for an easy getaway should he deem it necessary.

"What do those criminals look like?" Violet whispered.

He glanced across at her. "No one knows." Which was the difficulty. *How did you deal with criminals and eliminate them if their identity was unknown?* The truth of the matter was they couldn't. Hence his involvement. Andrew had tried to deal with the problem alone, but then they threatened to snatch Violet off the street if Andrew didn't comply. His first instinct was to contact Brandon, and he was so glad he did.

The train suddenly jolted, and they were soon on their way. Violet seemed to relax against him, and Brandon didn't complain. He glanced down at her and a shudder went down his spine. *Now that he'd had a taste of being with her, how would he survive when she was gone?* It was the very reason he'd kept his distance all this time.

He knew she would leave when all this madness was over. They'd shared more than a bed last night, but only because she was frightened. She needed comfort, someone to hold her, and he was in the right place at the right time. Otherwise, Violet wouldn't have given him the time of day.

The train suddenly jolted to a halt. *What was happening?* Brandon reached inside his jacket, his fingers gripping the gun he had hidden there. *Was it a train robbery, or something even more sinister?* He wanted to explore, but had no intention of leaving Violet alone. It could easily be a ruse to get him away from her, making her easy prey.

"Everything is all right, folks," the conductor said as he strolled along the carriage. "A tree has fallen across the tracks. We'll get moving again shortly."

Brandon grabbed Violet's hand. "Come with me," he commanded, pulling her along.

He felt her shudder under his grip. "Are we in trouble?" She sounded worried, not that he could blame her. Heck, he was afraid. Not for himself, but for his wife. This could easily be a ploy to get onto the train.

They made their way through each of the carriages until they were at the front. Brandon studied the area. Trees lined either side of the tracks, and as he suspected, it was a trick to get to Violet. Men were hidden behind the trees, but not well enough. Brandon had done this far too many times to miss the signs of an ambush.

He grabbed Violet's hand tighter and pulled her along, his gun now out of the holster and firmly in his grip. Running between the carriages slowed them down, and he knew his wife was terrified. He was terrified for her. *What if they got onto the train and did what they'd promised?* He swallowed down the emotion that threatened to overtake him and was determined not to let that happen.

"Keep the doors locked," he shouted to the conductor. "Don't let anyone inside." It wasn't only Violet's life at stake here, but the life of every passenger. He wouldn't put it past these criminals to kill everyone in sight. Anyone who would kill an innocent woman to get what they wanted would kill anyone in their path.

He heard Violet's intake of breath, but there was no time to console her. Brandon had to protect her, but how he would do that was anyone's guess. He silently prayed for the strength to get her through this ordeal. "What are we going to do?" Her quiet voice was disturbing.

Brandon turned to his wife. "We will get out of this, but I need you to keep up with me." She nodded, and they continued until they were near to the back of the train. They had two choices. The first was to go to the Pullman Car where he was certain Jonathan would give them entry, but was far more difficult for a criminal to gain entry.

The second choice was far more dangerous but also more effective. For this option, they needed to climb to the top of the train and lay down until it was safe to do otherwise. He quickly told Violet what they were doing and what it might mean. It could be hours before they could leave the roof of the train. She agreed to do whatever Brandon felt was best, and soon they were atop the train.

They heard gun fire, and Brandon prayed it was coming from the train being defended. He had one job, and that was to protect Violet. That was exactly what he would do.

What seemed like forever later, the train began to creep along. Brandon did not know what had changed to get them moving. He was far too grateful to analyze it.

“We should stay here until we arrive at the next station, and then we’re on the move again,” he whispered, not wanting to be overheard, despite their distance from anyone. Violet looked deflated, and it was apparent she was exhausted. He needed to find somewhere they could stay for a few days at least to allow her time to recover.

If they’d found her already, chances were they’d find her again.

It was pitch dark when Brandon felt himself being poked. “Brandon,” Violet whispered. “The train has stopped.” He was furious. Not with Violet, but with himself for falling asleep. He was supposed to be protecting her, and sleeping did not allow that to happen.

He glanced up at the starless sky. The moon sat behind clouds, which would allow them good coverage. Leaning over the side of the roof, it was difficult, but the lantern the station master carried allowed him to read the sign – they were at Angel's Bend.

He let out the breath he didn't realize he'd been holding. He'd been stationed here at one point which meant he knew his way around. "We're getting off here," he whispered, the cold air making his breath form little clouds. She nodded in the darkness, but didn't say a word.

Brandon climbed down the ladder first, and then Violet. Her agility surprised him, but knew he shouldn't be. She'd been afforded the best coaching money could buy in all the popular sports, including horse-riding. His wife was fit and able, despite her feisty temper.

She'd wrapped her skirts into her underwear to stop herself tripping on the steps, and it caught him off-guard. He momentarily stared at her ankles, and then her bare legs, then brought himself back to the task at hand. Andrew was going to be most displeased with him, and frankly, Brandon couldn't blame him. He'd been set one task – protect Violet – and instead had seduced her. It was most unprofessional of him.

Brandon had known the situation he'd put himself in by taking the assignment, but Andrew apparently had not.

His hands went around her waist as she neared the bottom rung of the ladder, and he pointed to a bush in the distance. "Run to there. I'll be right behind you." She followed his instructions and quickly hid. Moments later, the train moved with Brandon still on it. His heart pounded in his head. He had to get off, to join Violet, but couldn't risk being seen.

As the train moved past the station, he jumped, rolling down the hill toward the moving train. Now he risked being killed by the train. Violet needed him and he wouldn't be there. A week ago he wouldn't have cared, but now… Brandon was duty-bound to save his wife. Not to mention he'd dreamed of marrying her for as long as he could remember.

His arm reached out, and he grabbed hold of a small bush. He was less than a foot from the tracks, but that tiny plant saved his life. He held on for dear life, waiting for the train to pass. What Violet must think he had no idea. But he was certain she would be panicking by now.

It seemed like a lifetime before the train passed, but it was surely only minutes. He allowed himself to roll the rest of the way down the hill, and since he had no choice, hit the tracks with a thud. At the very least, he would have a massive bruise, at worst, a broken rib or two. He'd endured worse.

He lay on the damp ground momentarily to get his bearings, then headed back to where he'd directed his wife to hide. She must be beside herself with worry. The station was now in darkness except for a shimmer of light coming from beneath the door of the stationmaster's office. It suited him fine.

Fully expecting to find her gone, Brandon crept toward the bush he'd directed her too. But there she was, the dutiful wife, having done as she was told. If he was truthful with himself, Brandon was stunned. *Since when did Violet listen to what he told her? It was a rare event, but they found themselves in a unique situation. And if she'd left, where would she go?*

"Violet," he whispered into the darkness.

He heard her breath whoosh out of her mouth. "Praise the Lord!" she whispered, heavy emotion in her voice. "I was sure you were dead. Or still on the train." Despite the darkness, he noticed the tears shimmering on her eyelashes. He reached out and wiped them away. It seemed like such a simple thing to do, but felt far more intimate than he'd ever imagined. Another mark against him in Andrew's eyes.

He must stop thinking about Andrew and focus on Violet. She was the only person who mattered here.

She leaned her face into his hand, and Brandon pulled her close to him. "What do we do now?" she asked quietly.

It was a good question, and luckily, he had an idea.

Chapter Six

The sun was peaking over the horizon as they arrived at the abandoned ranch, and Violet took in the beauty of it. She was exhausted after having little sleep. Laying on the cold, hard surface of the train was not conducive to sleep. Although it hadn't stopped Brandon.

She was surprised, but decided he'd needed the sleep, so had left him. It wasn't as though anyone knew they were up there. More likely, the criminals trying to find her had concluded they'd left the train. In a way, they had.

"This is it," he said, as they continued toward the ranch. He grabbed her hand and ran, pulling her behind him. The entire time, he glanced about. *Did he think they may have been followed?* She swallowed down her fear and ran with him.

"Don't expect much. This place has been empty for a long time."

She shivered at the thought of wild creatures inhabiting the ranch, especially rats. The thought of rats terrified Violet more than the men trying to eliminate her. "What are we going to do for food?"

Brandon turned to her and smiled tentatively. "We'll work something out." He squeezed her hand and tugged her closer. Every time he did that she felt safe. He was her protector, that was why Andrew had contacted him, but it was more than that. Violet felt a change coming over her, and she wasn't sure what it was. Perhaps it was simply that Brandon had kept her out of danger, and for that she was grateful. She really had no idea.

They stood at the bottom of the steps leading up to the ranch entrance. "Be careful," he said, testing each step with his weight.

She followed carefully behind him and took each step slowly. When it came time to open the door, Brandon pushed her behind him, pulling his gun from his holster. "Stay here," he commanded, and fury burned inside her.

"I'd rather come inside with you," she said, glancing about. "I feel like a sitting duck out here." And she did. If the men trying to kill her were nearby, they'd have a clean shot, and she'd be dead in an instant. She might have led a sheltered life, but Violet knew enough to understand it was that simple.

He nodded and quickly opened the door, dragging her inside. Expecting birds and other wildlife to run in a flurry to escape, Violet was surprised by the absolute and utter silence. The ranch appeared to be in prestige condition, as though the owners had literally up and left the day before. Leaving everything as it was. Sure, there was dust, but apart from that, there was little disturbance.

Brandon reached a hand around her waist and pulled his wife close. "This is perfect," he whispered. Why he was whispering, she did not know. It was only the two of them, so no one else could hear. Although the pristine silence could evoke such a response.

She felt like an intruder and needed to know the circumstances. "What happened to the owners?"

He glanced down at her and swallowed. "They were both killed in an attempted stagecoach robbery. Mary-Ellen was almost eight months into her pregnancy." He shook his head. "It was an absolute tragedy." It was clear Brandon was still upset about their deaths from his expression. He tugged her along, and Violet followed him to the bedroom.

A double bed sat in the middle of the room, an intricately made quilt lay on it. The curtains were dusty, but matched the quilt beautifully. A cry escaped Violet as she noticed the crib sitting beside the bed. Tears fell from her eyes before she could stop them, and Brandon pulled her tight against him. "I'll get rid of it," he whispered. Violet heard him swallow back his own emotion, and she couldn't help but sob.

"I don't think I can stay here."

"We have no choice. Jacob and Mary-Ellen Hanson would insist if they were here." *Did that mean they were friends?* Violet was having a hard time with the circumstances, and she couldn't imagine what Brandon would be enduring. She nodded against his chest. "Are you all right?" She nodded again, afraid if she opened her mouth, another sob might escape.

He rubbed his hands over her back, then stepped forward and reached for the crib, carrying it out of the room. If he could move past the situation, then so could she. Violet pulled the quilt off the bed that appeared to be freshly made, taking it outside to shake off the dust. She would rinse the curtains – they should dry quickly with the wind that was picking up.

Feeling a little more confident, she wandered around the small ranch, exploring. There was a pantry, and it even had supplies in it. Not that she expected anything to be edible. After all this time, the flour was likely full of weevils, at the very least. The thought made her shudder.

"There's a root cellar out back." His voice behind her made Violet jump. "Sorry, I didn't mean to scare you. Anyway, I doubt any food we find here will be edible. Except maybe the vegetable garden out back, but that's probably dead by now."

Not that she knew much about gardening. They had someone to do that, but he was likely right. She would check anyway. Violet stepped further into the pantry and opened the pack of flour. Weevils scattered far and wide, causing her to screech. Brandon laughed. "That means the blighters will be in everything. I'll get rid of them." He scooped everything up and took it outside, saying he would burn it later.

She wandered into the kitchen. There was a good sized cookstove, and it even had wood sitting in it. A dusty kettle stood on top, and Violet wondered if they had left there it intending to make coffee when they returned home. She honestly didn't know how she would survive living in this place for even one night, let alone a longer term as Brandon had planned.

There was a fireplace in the sitting room with a large box full of chopped wood ready for burning. At least that was something they wouldn't need to worry about for a good while. It was obvious the couple led an idyllic life here until criminals who believed the world owed them, took it away.

Violet was startled by the sudden thought it was not unlike her own situation. Criminals had changed her world, too. They might not have killed her yet as they had the Hanson's but that was certainly their intention. It was then she realized Brandon was right – they would have wanted the pair to stay there and ensure their safety.

She opened the cookstove door, and, shoving in some old newspapers she found, lit the fire. She turned to the sink then. No taps. *What did they do for water?* It was then she noticed the bucket sitting at the side on the kitchen counter. She should have known – she'd noticed a small well out the back. It was clear to Violet staying here was going to be an experience she would never forget. Whether she survived the brutality of it was yet to be seen.

"I'll get that," Brandon said, taking the bucket from her hands. He was close behind her, and his body heat warmed her. It was all she could do not to turn and wrap her arms around him. He was comforting, and right now, she needed to know he was there. The moment this nightmare was over, they would go their separate ways, so she had to ignore those feelings. Especially knowing in her heart, she was only experiencing them because he was protecting her and keeping her safe.

She watched him at the well through the kitchen window. The glass was grubby, like everything else here, but she was grateful to have somewhere to stay, until it was no longer safe. The bed was clean and comfortable, the fire would warm them, and they were isolated. According to Brandon, they could stay here for at least a few days. Perhaps even longer, provided they weren't discovered.

The back door slammed, and Violet jumped. She was far too jittery for her own good and needed to stop being so fearful. "Are you all right?" Brandon's hand reached out and touched her shoulder and a shiver went down her spine.

"I think so." She rinsed the kettle, then filled it with fresh water from the well. It would be some time before it boiled. Then a thought hit her. "We don't have tea or coffee. Or food. Or anything," she said, close to panicking.

"Let's check the root cellar before we worry." Ever the voice of calm, he took her hand and led Violet to the root cellar. It was at the side of the house, and if you didn't know it was there, you could totally miss it. It was secured with a rusty padlock, and Brandon swore under his breath. "Sorry," he said, then headed into the small shed not far away. Returning with some tools, he attempted to open the padlock, and eventually, after what seemed forever, succeeded.

Violet climbed the few steps down into the cellar and glanced about. Various types of food sat on the shelves, but would they be edible? Like the garden, it was doubtful. She shivered, and Brandon wrapped an arm around her. Little did he know it wasn't only the cold that made her tremble, but the thought she was stealing from the dead.

There was a large tin of coffee, as well as a small bag of tea. She knew the tea would be spoiled after all this time, but being sealed in tin, the coffee was likely fine. There was salted meat, which she had her suspicions would not be usable, along with potatoes and other root vegetables. She gathered up the tea and coffee, some of the meat, and enough potatoes for supper. All the time, keeping an open mind about their usefulness. As they were leaving, Violet spotted some tins of condensed milk. No doubt an emergency supply for the baby. She forced herself not to cry and snatched up one tin.

Between them, all the food they'd chosen was taken into the kitchen, where they decided what was usable and what wasn't. The salted meat appeared to be fine, as Brandon believed it would be. Tea was stale, but the vegetables were still usable, but barely.

Violet made them each a mug of coffee after washing the dusty crockery. She longed for tea, but it was out of her control. She had begun to realize this could easily be a long-term situation, and she needed to come to terms with it.

"Lucky for us, the coffee is still as fresh as the day they purchased it," Brandon said, a smile on his face. "Too bad about the tea. Make a list of the supplies we need and I'll go into town later."

Violet gasped at the revelation. "You can't leave me here alone," she almost shrieked, trying to keep herself calm.

He reached across the table and covered her hand. "No one knows we're here. The ranch is so far from everything, most people don't know it even exists. Besides, you can hide in the root cellar."

She shivered at the thought. "Won't you be recognized? Apart from your scruffy appearance, that is."

Brandon rubbed a hand across his chin. It had been several days since he'd shaved. Normally, he'd be annoyed, but it might be the disguise he needed. The last thing he wanted was to be followed back to the ranch and put Violet in danger. "It might be enough to hide my true identity," he said as he continued to rub at his chin.

"Did you hear that?" Violet asked, surprise in her voice.

Brandon stared at her. "Hear what?"

"Chickens. How would there be chickens still here?"

"They're scavengers. If there's food, they would hang around." Brandon shoved his chair back and ran outside, Violet following behind him. The chicken coop was far from the house, but the chickens were near the house. "Likely they heard movement and were curious." He grinned then. "Chickens means eggs, but we'll need to search for them. They haven't been locked up for a year or more, so they would have laid anywhere and everywhere."

He counted eight chickens, but they scurried all over the place, meaning it could be more. Or less. It was hard to tell when they wouldn't stand still. "I found one," Violet called to him. "Oh, and another!" She walked carefully, ensuring not to stand on any eggs that might be in amongst the long grass.

"There must be feed somewhere here," Brandon said, "otherwise they'd have either left or died." He headed toward the shed again, but there was no feed. Checking the chicken coop, there was a shelf where a bag of feed was stored. It was less than a quarter full. A hole was pecked into the corner, and the feed slowly drained out. "That would be funny if it wasn't so clever," he said.

On their way back to the house, they found more eggs. "I guess that's breakfast. I'm starving," Violet said. "I don't know about you."

"Famished. The coffee helped, but it doesn't fill an empty belly." She figured he was used to it. Being a marshal, he was likely caught out in the middle of nowhere on a regular basis.

Arriving back at the house, they heard clattering inside. Violet's heart rate sped up, and she was petrified. They left the eggs at the back door, and Brandon pushed her behind him, clinging to her hand. It was reassuring to know he had no intention of leaving her alone.

He pulled his gun from its holster and headed inside. There was no one to be seen, but there, across the other side of the sitting was a rooster. They breathed a collective sigh of relief. "Remind me not to leave the door open again," Brandon said, as he tried to hold back his laughter. Violet noticed him staring out of the front window as he spoke. All seemed calm, and no one was about. Suddenly, he leaned down and snatched up the boisterous rooster, who was none too happy to be held.

Once gone, the house was peaceful again, but Brandon checked all the rooms, anyway. It was the most excitement Violet wanted to have to deal with for some time to come.

She glanced about. The ranch was well built and tidy. It really only needed a sweep and dusting. She would explore properly while Brandon was gone. It was going to be their home for goodness knew how long, and she wanted to make the most of it.

Sleeping in the Hanson's bed would not be a simple task, but there was little choice. There was a second bedroom, but they had used it for storage, and had no bed in it. Besides, Brandon was her legal husband, which meant there was no chance of ruining her reputation. She decided there and then to enjoy their time at the ranch as much as possible.

Chapter Seven

The last thing Brandon wanted was to leave Violet alone at the Hanson's ranch, but he had little choice. Anyone seeing them together might have their suspicions, especially if someone had been asking around. This way, it may not arouse suspicions as easily.

He'd already decided to stick to the few stores he needed to visit. Even then, it was risky as many of the folks living in Angel's Bend when he was last there knew Brandon. His only hope was his unruly hair and scruffy beard. It had been a long walk into town, but he would visit the livery while he was there. He was more than thankful Andrew had slipped that wad of money into Violet's reticule before the wedding. Thank goodness she'd had the foresight to keep a tight hold of it throughout their ordeal. He'd planned to stay at his parents' hotel for the duration, but that plan went awry quickly.

He felt ready to collapse by the time he stepped inside the mercantile. It was always going to be an issue, but the moment he stepped inside, his greatest fear came to fruition. "Buck! Marsh…"

Brandon put his fingers to his lips, then whispered. “Please don’t say it, Lloyd. I’m here incognito.”

The other man frowned momentarily, then appeared enlightened. “Welcome to Angel’s Bend, Sir. What can I do for you today?”

Brandon passed over his list. “I have other tasks to fulfill, and will be back shortly.” He immediately left the store for the livery and hoped there were new owners. The more people who recognized him, the more risk there was to Violet. As he approached, the first thing he noticed was the sign. *Harper’s Livery,* it said, and he let go of the breath he didn’t know he was holding. Last time he was here, Arthur Lonigan owned the livery.

He strode in, confident of not being recognized here. Best-case scenario, a wagon and two horses would suit them best, but it depended on the cost. There might be a wad of money available, but it would likely need to last quite some time. He couldn’t afford to be wasteful with Andrew’s money.

Standing to one side stood a used wagon, and Brandon headed straight for it, checking it over. An older man wandered toward him, giving Brandon time to do a complete inspection. “It’s a good wagon. Sturdy,” the man said. “Jack Harper. I own this place.” He extended his hand, and they shook hands.

"I'm looking for a sturdy wagon. Something that will carry supplies more than anything." Brandon rubbed at his chin. His beard was annoying him. "Do you have any horses for sale? I'll need at least one, but preferably two."

Harper pulled two horses out of their stalls and Brandon checked them over. He wasn't an expert on horses, but had owned enough of them to know magnificent horses when he saw them. "What do you want for the horses and wagon? I'll need reins and harnesses as well."

"Run into Indians, did you?"

Brandon had to think quickly. "I was set upon by robbers. Lost both horses in the assault. Darn shame too, they were splendid horses." He pulled his hat off his head for a second or two. "They were good at shooting horses, but I'm a far better shot. Still, I had to walk quite a distance to get here," he added.

"That is a shame." Jack thought for a moment, then offered a figure that seemed reasonable. They shook on it and Brandon pulled out his wallet. He purposely didn't take all the money with him, only what he felt would be necessary. If he truly had been attacked by robbers, they'd be left with nothing.

Once he'd paid, he was handed a receipt for his purchases. Everyone in town knew him as Buck, so using his real name would hopefully keep his identity secret. Worse case scenario, he could say he was Buck's cousin, their surnames being the same.

He hitched up the horses to the wagon and was soon on his way. He headed back to the mercantile, then went on to the feed store. The horses would need feed, and it wouldn't be long before he'd need to replace the chicken feed. It was a miracle it had lasted that long.

Ideally, they needed a cow for milk, but not knowing how long they'd be there, he refrained. Violet had listed condensed milk as one of the purchases, and that would sustain them for some time. His plan was to stay at the ranch as long as they could. It was isolated from other ranches in the area, and everyone who knew about it believed the Hanson's ranch to be abandoned. Since Jacob and Mary-Ellen had no living family, they wouldn't be suddenly evicted.

He made some meagre purchases at the butcher shop and could finally head home. He'd spent a pretty penny of Violet's wad of money, but this was exactly the sort of thing Andrew had intended it to be used for. Both men had known the newlyweds could be off the grid for a long period.

Brandon was relieved when the ranch was in sight. He'd been sure not to be followed, but was most displeased to see Violet on the porch sweeping away the dirt. *What if she was spotted?* He knew it was unlikely, even so, one never knew who might stumble across the property.

"I told you to stay in the root cellar and out of sight," he said between clenched teeth.

She shrugged. "It was too cold down there and I had no intention of wasting good time when I could clean the house." She waved a hand in front of her face. "It was way too dusty."

He couldn't argue with that. The place *was* full of dust. "I got everything on your list." The last thing he wanted was to have a disagreement. They were stuck with each other until this was all over. How they would know Violet was safe again, he had no idea. It may end up being a problem.

He jumped into the back of the wagon and handed the lightest supplies to Violet, saving the heaviest items for himself. "Remind me not to walk into town again," he said as he chuckled. "I was so relieved when I secured this lot." He waved his hands toward the horses and wagon. "And my feet are killing me. I think I have blisters on my blisters."

"I'll bet," she said, then took the supplies inside. With everything finally unloaded, he drove the horses into the barn. The building was in need repairs, but was solid and would keep the horses out of the weather and away from harm. They could be there only means of escape if things went awry.

It was eerie standing in the barn as he brushed horses. Memories came flooding back and despite trying to fight them back, he couldn't forget happier times he'd stood here doing exactly the same thing, with Jacob by his side. They'd become good friends from the moment they'd met. Mary-Ellen's father built the ranch from the ground up. When he passed, Jacob inherited it. There was a rather small mortgage, which Jacob paid in record time. The ranch was prosperous and earned a good income.

Being so far out of town, Brandon liked to check up on them from time to time, ensuring they were safe. In the process, he'd become close to the pair.

He swallowed back the sadness that was threatening to overtake him.

The last thing he did for the couple after the absolute tragedy of their untimely deaths, was to ensure the livestock was divided between the neighboring ranchers. With no family and no heirs, there was little choice. The last thing Jacob would have wanted was to have the livestock to die of starvation.

Within months of their demise, Brandon was given another assignment, in another town. He hadn't returned to Angel's Bend until now.

"Coffee's ready," Violet called from the entrance of the barn. It was the distraction he needed. His thoughts had become far too morbid, and it was getting to him.

"Coming." He finished brushing the second horse before heading to the house. Opening the front door, the aroma of food cooking hit his senses. "Something smells good. I didn't know you could cook." He stepped toward Violet and wrapped his arms around her. She was the distraction he needed, and he felt comforted by her presence.

She laughed, and the tinkling sound warmed his soul. "I found a cookbook in a kitchen drawer. Just as well or we might starved. I hope you like pound cake."

"Mary-Ellen always had a fresh pound cake when she knew I was visiting," he said, memories hitting him yet again.

"I'm sorry. You obviously knew them well. Being here must be painful."

He nodded then. *How could he deny the truth?* It was tough, and undeniably painful, but he had to endure it for Violet's sake. She placed a mug of coffee in front of him, and a plateful of the warm cake in the center of the table. "It's good," he said once he emptied his mouth.

“How do pancakes sound for supper? I’ll cook fried potatoes to go with them. Tomorrow I’ll make a stew, but there’s not enough time today.”

“Sounds good. There’s plenty to do around here to keep us both busy for a long time.” Brandon knew it to be true. The biggest test, for both of them, was sleeping in Thomas and Mary-Ellen’s bed. Taking the crib up to the loft was one of the hardest things he’d ever had to do. Thomas had been so proud of his handiwork, and had it sat next to their bed in waiting since the day it was ready. Finding their limp bodies amongst the wreckage was something he would never forget.

“I wish we could go for a stroll. It would do us both some good,” Violet said. It was as though she could read his mind and knew exactly the way his thoughts were heading.

“We could, but we can’t stray too far.” He drank down the rest of his coffee then reached for his jacket and hat. “You’ll need a coat. There is sure to be one in the wardrobe.”

“On second thought,” she said, her expression suddenly sad.

“They were dear friends of mine,” he whispered. “They would want us to avail ourselves of anything we needed.” Brandon knew it to be true. They were the nicest, most kind-hearted people he’d ever met, and was certain they would not want their ranch go to ruin. Or their belongings left to rot.

He followed her into the bedroom and watched as Violet searched through Mary-Ellen's clothes. He realized she was more than a little distressed at the prospect of wearing his dead friend's clothes. "I'll have to do the same thing," he said quietly. "Our luggage is still on the train."

She turned to face him. "In all the chaos, I'd forgotten about it." She scowled then, distorting her pretty face. "I bought several new outfits. So annoying!"

Brandon laughed at her antics, and it helped lift his spirits. "At least you didn't use any of the money Andrew planted in your reticule."

"That was Andrew? I assumed it was Mother." Realization hit her then. "Wait, how do you know that?"

"I checked your bank account." He could see the revelation was both annoying and frustrating to his new wife, but they had to ensure they found her. Accessing her bank account confirmed exactly where he would find her. He'd only just left the bank at Shady Glen when she turned up with her new friends. "Enough of that. Did you find a coat?"

"No, but I found a woolen shawl. That will have to do."

They left through the back and headed past the chicken coop. Brandon could now see there were far more chickens than he'd first thought. It was probably a good thing since it meant they would have plenty of eggs, and could also kill a chicken or two for food.

He spotted more eggs, and would collect them on the way back. "We can't go too far, otherwise we might be seen by neighboring ranchers." It was highly unlikely since the nearest neighbor was close to ten miles away, but he wanted to keep Violet on her toes. "Besides, it won't be long and darkness will set in."

They walked in silence until they stood at the top of a small hill. "It's beautiful up here," Violet proclaimed, turning to take in the entire area. "I don't think I've ever seen anything as magnificent as this before."

That summed up what he'd told Jacob the first time he'd been there, too. Violet was already far too affected by just being in their home and he had no intention of adding to her anguish. "It certainly is." Speaking only those words was heartbreaking. He dearly wanted to tell her everything about his friends and their land, but refrained for both their sakes. "We should return soon," he said as he grabbed her hand and headed toward the house again.

Snatching up the eggs they found along the way meant they'd have plenty for the next day or two. Certainly enough for the pancakes Violet intended to make for supper tonight.

Brandon had always preferred the simple life, but knew it was not for Violet. She'd been brought up in the biggest house in the county, the best food, and with servants to bend to her every need. The family had a team of cooks, and when Violet needed clothes, they summoned the family seamstress. For her sake, he hoped they did not have to stay here long.

For his sake, he hoped they did. He wanted nothing more than a genuine marriage with his childhood crush.

They had both put it off far too long.

Violet fussed about the kitchen – first cleaning up from supper, then cleaning every countertop, whether it needed scrubbing or not. Next came the table, and then she swept.

Brandon cleaned the fireplace, despite having done it the night before. He restacked the wood, checked no one was loitering outside, ensured all the doors were locked, and closed all the curtains. Finally, neither of them could put if off any longer.

His heart thudded at the thought of what lay ahead. Normally it would be an easy task – going to bed usually was. But tonight, knowing he would be sleeping in Thomas and Mary-Ellen's bed, his heart ached.

Violet was pale at the prospect, and he guessed his face would be equally colorless. She stood slumped at the sink, head down, shoulders sagged. There was nothing else for it, they simply had to head to the bedroom and go to bed.

He came up behind his wife, and put an arm around her. "We can't put it off any longer," he whispered as though the spirits of his dead friends would hear. "Both of us need to sleep. Who knows what the days ahead will bring?"

She nodded as though she knew what he said was true. Brandon also knew once they'd slept in the bed, it would be far easier. At least he hoped it would. He turned his back while Violet readied herself for bed, only turning around when she said he could. He removed his clothes, with only his drawers remaining, and tucked his gun under the pillow.

"Ready?" They'd agreed to pull back the bedding at the same time. Each knowing how difficult this was going to be for the other. Except Violet didn't know his friends. Having a personal relationship with them added yet another layer of angst for Brandon.

They each sat on the side of the bed – the side they'd each agreed would be *their side* for the duration – then tossed their legs up onto the bed. So far so good. Brandon reached over and held Violet's hand tightly, his heart pounding the entire time.

This last part would be telling. The pair leaned forward and held tight to the bedding, pulling it up over themselves as they slid down into the bed ready for sleep. The moment their heads hit the pillow, he heard pitiful cries coming from Violet, her face against the pillow. If he wasn't a marshal, someone sent to protect her, he might have done the same.

Brandon slid across the bed and pushed himself tight against her, wrapping her in his arms. Tomorrow night would be easier. He'd keep telling himself that, but it didn't mean it would work.

Chapter Eight

Those first few days at the ranch were challenging, but Violet enjoyed the peace of Angel's Bend. Brandon had been on edge initially, but seemed a little more relaxed now. Violet knew he would still be vigilant, despite his outward appearance.

She stared through the kitchen window, enjoying the scene in front of her. Getting up at the break of day to let the chickens out was a novel experience, but one she'd easily fallen into. Collecting eggs and making them into something tangible was something Violet never thought possible. Let alone do it herself.

It hadn't taken long to realize this was a lifestyle Brandon loved and had previously enjoyed. After some questioning, she'd discovered he'd lived in this area for quite some time. No wonder he was worried about going into town.

"You are becoming quite the cook," Brandon said, breaking into her thoughts.

She chuckled, amused that she could be anything close to a good cook. "Mary-Ellen's recipes have certainly helped." The amusement all but died on her lips. Violet hadn't allowed herself to think about the couple whose home they'd overtaken. Brandon insisted they would be ecstatic about their presence. She wasn't convinced.

She hadn't heard him move from the table, and startled as his arms came up around her. "I promise you, they would be glad we're here. Not under these circumstances, but they would hate knowing the home they built with their own hands stood unoccupied all this time."

Violet leaned back into him. Deep in her heart, she knew he was right. It was an absolute tragedy that a beautiful home like this, and with all this wonderful land, stood empty. To leave it this way was appalling. She could only imagine what the deceased couple would think.

As much as she had loathed Brandon at the start of their marriage, she had found it in her heart to forgive him. Believing he was the one behind her forced marriage, she was furious, but finding out it was Andrew was even worse. *Why didn't he tell her the truth?* She would have refused – that was why. It was time to put aside her anger and forgive both men involved. After all, they were concerned about her, and endeavoring to keep her safe from harm. Still, they could have gone about it differently.

"You seem to be settling in," Brandon said, then leaned in and kissed her neck. *They had become closer in recent days, but what else did she expect?* Living in the same house, with little chance of going anywhere, of course they would get to know each other better. And with only one bed…

From what Brandon had said, Andrew would be infuriated, Well, too bad for him. Her brother was the one who dreamed up the entire scenario. Planned it to ensure she was kept in the dark about the dangers. Thank goodness Brandon had told her the truth or she would still be none the wiser. She had to give him credit for that. Few people had the gumption to go against a Southerby. Being Andrew's closest friend since childhood, Brandon saw him differently.

"I'm glad you're my wife," he whispered as he continued to nibble at her neck. "I want you to know it didn't take much convincing on my part."

Violet's eyes opened wide in astonishment. "You wanted to deceive me?"

His grip tightened around her, and his head shot up. "I didn't mean…"

"You were totally in cahoots with my brother. You are both accountable in my book." Fury burned up inside her.

Brandon turned her around in his arms. She was so angry her face hurt, and it was all she could do to fight back her tears. It appeared they were becoming something close to friends. At least they tolerated each other. During the day anyway.

He stared into her face. First staring into her eyes, then his gaze moved to her lips. For a moment, Violet thought he might kiss her. Not that she wanted him to. Oh no, that would be a punishment too awful to bear.

Her heart fluttered at the mere thought of it.

"You must know," he whispered, all the time gazing at her lips, "I have loved you from the day we met."

"So you've said." Her words were harsh – he deserved her wrath.

"Andrew warned me off."

She stiffened. *Why did her brother think he had control over her life?* "And of course, you do everything he tells you to do." She was referring to that kiss. The one he stole in the garden all those years ago, and was certain he would understand.

"He never let me visit the house again after that day. So yes, I guess I did. But not any more. I agreed to marry you to keep you from harm." She should be grateful, but his words only made Violet more angry than she already was. "I couldn't bear the thought of anyone else marrying you. Of putting their hands on you."

He looked so sad, and she should feel sorry for him, but she didn't. Instead, she pounded his chest with her fists. "How dare you! You and Andrew are both.... I hate you both!"

Tears rolled down her cheeks. She was far more incensed than she could ever remember being.

Brandon grabbed her wrists to stop the pounding. She would leave a dent on his pride, nothing more, but it was likely annoying him. Instead of pushing her away as she suspected he would, Brandon leaned down and kissed her. Not a peck on the cheek, or a chaste kiss to the forehead, but he kissed her full on the lips. Her heart fluttered to the extent she felt light-headed. A tingle went down her spine, and she couldn't help but kiss him back.

Brandon suddenly jumped back. "Someone is coming," he said, totally on alert. "Hide in the bedroom, under the bed. Keep hidden until I say otherwise. And don't move a muscle."

He grabbed her by the arm and herded her into the bedroom, shutting the door behind her. More than anything, she felt confusion surrounding her. She heard nothing. *How was it that Brandon heard a noise that was non-existent to her?*

Soon, there was a knock on the door. *Would he answer or just ignore the visitor?* One thing she could be certain of, and that was his hand would be tightly gripped on the gun he carried on his chest.

To her surprise, Violet soon heard low mutterings. Next thing she knew, the bedroom door was opened and Brandon was telling her to come out from hiding.

He reached for her hand and helped Violet to her feet. She was beyond surprised to see a stranger standing in front of her.

Her heart pounded with fear and her entire body shook. *Was this the end?*

The relief was palpable. Brandon was certain things were about to heat up. To see a friendly face was the last thing he expected.

"Violet," he said, watching her carefully. She was beyond pale and white as a ghost. Would she faint? "Meet an old friend of mine, Sheriff Earl Jacobsen."

"I think I need to sit down," she said, her voice shaking. Brandon picked her up and carried her to the sitting room. "I could have walked," she said, poking at his chest.

If he was honest with himself, he didn't think she could. The way she looked, he was certain he was about to pick her up off the floor. His own brain should have told him to warn her. Of course she'd be scared of a complete stranger. *What else did he expect to happen?* Now Brandon was annoyed with himself, but his wife was his priority.

"I was riding past and saw the smoke from the chimney," the sheriff told her. "Since the… accident, this place has been empty. Thought I'd better check it out. The last person I expected to find was Marshal Buck Honeywell. Heard there was a stranger passing through town too. I can see how no one recognized you." He grinned then, but Brandon knew better.

"It didn't fool Lloyd. At the mercantile," he explained for Violet's sake. "He recognized me immediately. Luckily, he understood my need for anonymity. No explanation needed."

Earl frowned. "He didn't tell me."

"Of course not. I asked him not to tell anyone." He glanced across at Violet. She had a little color in her face now, so that had to be a good sign. Brandon stood. "Do you have time for coffee?"

The other man laughed. "There's always time for coffee. Besides, I think we should talk."

Violet stood then, despite Brandon's protest. "I'm fine now. It was the shock of seeing a stranger standing there."

She hurried into the kitchen and poured each man a mug of coffee. She cut up the leftovers of yesterday's cake and placed it in front of them. Then she went outside. Brandon knew she was scared, but she'd tried to hide it. Most of the time she did, but now and then he saw through her façade. He didn't blame her one bit. Her situation was not a good one, and until they caught the blackmailers, she would never be safe. The trouble was, being out here in the middle of nowhere, he did not know the situation back in Rusty Hollow. Nor did he have a clue of how to find out.

"Let me do some checking," Earl said. "I can ask around and let you know the outcome."

"No!" Brandon turned on his long-time friend. "If you do that, they will work out where we are. We'll stay low here for as long as I feel it's necessary."

"You've already been here around a week, from what I've deduced."

"Something like that. I've lost track of time, to be honest."

Earl grinned. "I've no doubt, especially with a pretty little thing like Violet."

"Easy. That's my wife you're talking about." Brandon was becoming annoyed. Wife or not, he didn't like Earl checking her out.

The sheriff put his hands up in front of him. "Slow down. I did not know. When did this happen?"

Good question. Brandon had to think about that – so much had happened since the wedding. "Two weeks, three weeks maybe? It's been such a tumultuous time, I don't honestly know."

Now Earl looked confused. "Let me get this right – your friend's sister was in danger, so you married her? What kind of crazy logic is that?" He scratched his head. "I guess you know what you're doing."

"I guess I do," he almost snarled, then backed down. *When did he get so defensive about Violet?* He knew the answer – long before he was an adult.

"Well, I'll be off. I'll check on you from time to time. Do you need supplies? I can bring them with me next time."

"We're right for now, but to be truthful, I doubt we'll still be here in a few days. If we keep moving, it could be safer."

"Or not," Earl added. "This place is incredibly isolated, and no one comes out this way unless they're headed here. You should know that. Folks who are new to town don't even know it exists."

Either his brain was scrambled from having Violet around, or he simply wasn't thinking. Earl was right. The road to the Hanson property was not a thoroughfare. A person had to deviate off the main road to get here, so it was highly unlikely they'd have unwanted visitors. "That being the case, why did you come here?"

"Just a hunch. Knowing it was abandoned, it was the first place that came to mind."

The backdoor slammed, and Brandon stood. Violet was joining them, and the last thing he wanted was for her to hear them talk about the dangers surrounding her. "It's so peaceful here. I could stay forever," she said.

She was glowing. The sunshine and fresh air were doing her good, and were far better than the smoke-filled skies of home. Rusty Hollow had once been a quiet little town, but now it was full of factories and industrial plants. The serenity was no longer there.

Violet came and stood by his side and a calmness came over him. She glanced up and smiled, and it warmed his heart.

"Well, I'll be off. Thanks for your hospitality, Mrs. Honeywell." The sheriff tipped his hat and headed toward the door.

Brandon hoped Earl was not spotted returning to town. He prayed their existence was not revealed. The outcome may not be a good one.

He stood at the window, Violet by his side, and watched as his friend rode away.

Chapter Nine

What Earl said had made perfect sense, and they stayed put. His friend had visited more than once, and bought supplies with him each time. Brandon couldn't believe it had now been several months since they'd arrived, but the more time they spent together, the closer he and Violet had become. He certainly wouldn't complain about that.

Still, he would prefer if his wife was in love with him, as he was with her. There were no signs of her feeling that way, but he could live with that. They were happy together, and that was the main thing. He pained him that he wasn't sure she'd feel the same after the danger to her was over. He hadn't mentioned the situation again, and neither had she. It was something neither of them wanted to think about.

He stared at her through the kitchen window as she hung washing out. She'd become very domesticated, and seemed far more happy now than when they'd first arrived. To Brandon, it felt as though this was their home, and their property, but he knew that wasn't the case. There would come a day when they would have to give it all up.

That could also be the day they parted ways.

The thought left him with a hollow feeling. A sense of complete and utter loss. Whether that was because he risked losing Violet, or whether it was the house he would mourn the loss of, he wasn't certain. He shook his head and admonished himself. Brandon knew, no matter the outcome, it was Violet he couldn't bear to lose.

She waved to him from outside, and his heart fluttered. Chickens crowded about her, and she chased them away, laughing the entire time. When they'd first arrived, she was afraid of them, but now they were almost friends. The fact she fed them each day might have something to do with that.

He turned at the sound of the horses making a racket, and he was immediately on alert. It didn't seem long since Earl had been, so it was unlikely to be him.

Brandon ran to the front windows to see the horses running around the paddock filled with fear. There was no one in sight. The back door slammed, and he knew Violet had heard it, too.

"What's going on?"

"No idea. Stay put." He waved her into the bedroom and shut the door. Then gingerly watched outside again. The horses were still going crazy, and there was still no one in sight. That could only mean one thing – rattle snakes. In the entire time they'd been here, he'd not spotted a single rattle snake. Until today. Horses were petrified of them.

He ran outside, glancing about as he did, ensuring it wasn't a ruse. Then pulled his gun from its holster. Before anything else, he would lead the horses to safety. It would mean putting himself in danger, but so be it. He grabbed Doby by his halter, and then Rocky, pulling them both toward the barn. Once safely inside, he returned to the paddock. He would eliminate those critters if it was the last thing he ever did.

Two shots later, and two dead rattle snakes.

As he headed back to the ranch house, he heard the screaming. He ran quicker than he'd ever moved before. *Was it a ploy after all, to get him away from the house?* The front door was barely open before he was inside. The bedroom door was still closed, which confused him. Gun in hand, he slowly opened the door. Violet sat on the side of the bed, sobbing.

"Violet?" His voice was gentle, despite the pounding of his erratic heart. "Are you hurt?"

She glanced up then, surprise on her face. "Brandon? I thought you were…" She didn't continue, but put her face in her hands and sobbed again. "The gunshots. I thought they'd come and had killed you." He sat on the bed beside her and wrapped his terrified wife in his arms.

"With all the screaming, I thought they'd come for you. We are a good pair," he said, then chuckled. Not that it was a laughing matter, especially with Violet so upset, but he was far more relieved than he ever thought possible. "I've decided Earl is right. We're safe here. No one but long-time residents of Angel's Bend are even aware of the existence of this property, and many of those who did, are long buried. We could stay here the rest of our lives, and no one would be any the wiser." He cradled her in his arms, and eventually she calmed down. Only moments earlier, she'd been outside and happy as could be. It proved to Brandon how life could change in an instant.

That night, Violet was still unsettled, and he held her in his arms as they lay in bed. As always, his pistol lay under his pillow. Brandon couldn't stay awake twenty-four hours a day, so it was the next best thing. His arms wrapped around her. He was where he wanted to be – with the only woman he had ever loved. The pity of it was she didn't love him back. He truly wished she did, his life would be perfect then.

He listened to the birds outside their window. He loved waking up to the sounds of birds chirping in the morning, and the rooster signaling it was time to get up. The peacefulness of this location was something he would truly miss when Violet was safe again. He only wished they could stay here forever more. It would be a wonderful place to bring up children.

If he owned this property, it would again be filled with livestock, and he would have ranch hands, as Jacob did. It had been a busy and prosperous ranch, and there was no reason it couldn't be again. He closed his eyes against the thought, knowing it would never come to fruition. Even if the ranch had been for sale, he could never afford it. Better not to think about it.

Violet quietly groaned in her sleep, and it made him smile. To think only months ago, she was totally out of his reach. *And now?* She lay at ease in his arms. It wasn't one-sided, as he felt more content now than he had for a long time. Years, if he was honest with himself.

As she rolled over, his hands landed on her stomach. "Violet?" he whispered. "Are you all right? Are you sick?"

She turned to face him, pulling his hands to her stomach. "I guess you felt that." She smiled at him when it happened again.

"We're…" he couldn't find the words. He was so shocked at the revelation. "We're having a baby?" His heart filled with joy, and he pulled his wife to him and kissed her. "Why didn't you tell me before?"

"I needed to be certain." He grinned down at her. In all his years, with the work he undertook, Brandon never believe he would become a father. He held her tight as they lay together in the bed. "I love you more than you'll ever know," he whispered. Her silence told him all he needed to know.

As the months went by, Brandon was tempted to contact Andrew. But deep in his heart, he didn't want to let go of Violet. He knew it was wrong, but he loved her more now than he ever had. Their proximity to each other likely to blame.

It was incredibly selfish of him, Brandon knew that, but how could he continue to live without his wonderful wife in his life? Not to mention the baby they'd created together. They lived peacefully and happily on the ranch together, and neither wanted to leave. Not once had Violet asked to go back to Rusty Hollow. She still hadn't completely forgiven Andrew for his deception and had said as much. They were both keenly aware she would never have married Brandon under other circumstances, and that pained him greatly.

Violet waddled in from feeding the chickens and near collapsed in a chair. She was fiercely independent, and short of demanding she rest, he had no way to stop her doing chores.

"You look plum worn out," Brandon told her, pouring Violet a cup of tea. "The baby must be close now?" She'd refused to go into town for the doc to check her over, and he totally understood her reluctance. Sheriff Earl Jacobsen had brought the doc to the ranch under the threat of secrecy. Doc was more concerned about Violet than anything else.

That was a few weeks ago, by Brandon's reckoning – it was easy to lose track of time out here. Earl was due back any day, and would bring supplies with him.

It was easy to lose themselves out here. The peace and quiet away from other people was bliss. Not once had Brandon missed his previous life. Being moved from town to town just as he settled in to a new home, traveling all over the county; he missed none of it.

Right now, he was the happiest he'd been for as long as he could remember. Violet stood, and groaned. He was quickly by her side, helping her into the bedroom when her waters broke. Tears rolled down her face. "The baby is coming." She glanced up at him. "What are we going to do? I don't want to lose this baby." She gripped him by the shirt and cried against his chest.

"That will not happen," he said firmly. "I'll ride into town and get the doc."

Her look of terror had him reconsidering, but there was no other choice. “Please Brandon, don’t leave me alone.” His heart thudded. It was the last thing he wanted to do, but he didn’t want to lose his wife and baby. It left him without options.

He slip his hands under her and carried his wife to the bedroom, laying her gently on the bed. “I’m sorry, Violet, there isn’t a choice. I have to fetch the doctor.”

She scowled at him then. “Please don’t leave me.” She reached for his hand, and Brandon sat down beside her, his heart ripped in two.

A knock at the door interrupted them. He sighed with relief, praying it was his friend come to visit. Brandon could send him to fetch the doctor.

He leaned in and kissed his wife gently, then left the room. He yanked the front door open to let him in. “Earl, Doc. You do not know how relieved I am to see you both.”

Earl’s arms were full of supplies, and the doc carried his black medical bag. “You’re going to need that,” he said, pointing at the bag. “Violet’s water has broken.”

The doctor rushed inside, almost knocking Brandon over in the process.

Brandon paced the floor for far too many hours. His wife's screams were more than he could take, and he left the house and went outside. Since the incident with the rattle snakes, he'd carefully checked the paddocks daily, ensuring the horses were kept safe. Doby and Rocky had become like family, along with the cow Earl had brought to them a few months ago as soon as he'd discovered Violet's condition.

He wandered about, Earl by his side. "She will be fine. Doc's good at what he does."

Brandon stared at him, hoping and silently praying his friend was right. "I should have taken her into town for regular checks. It's too isolated out here."

Earl slapped him on the back. "Doc was happy to come out here and check on her." He followed Brandon to the barn, where he wandered about doing nothing in particular, except keeping himself occupied.

"We both love it here, and yet, in some ways, it feels as though Violet is being kept in a prison."

Earl stared at him in amazement. "She loves it here as much as you do. You only have to look at her to know that."

Warmth flooded him. Brandon had suspected as much, but she'd never voiced her thoughts on it. Nor had she told him she loved him, and they were the only words he wanted to hear. Yes, they were legally married, but she'd been forced into it. There was no forcing on his part, but he felt guilty for his part in the deception. Even if it was done to save her life.

"Brandon, get yourself up here!" Doc stood on the porch, calling out to him. "I need your help."

His heart sank. *Did that mean Violet and the baby were in trouble?* He ran faster than he'd ever ran before, leaving Earl behind. "Are they…?" He couldn't bring himself to say the words.

"They're fine. Since I don't have my nurse out here, I need you to do her job." He slapped Brandon on the back. "That baby will arrive any minute now."

Brandon gulped. "Any minute?"

"Pull yourself together. I need towels, lots of them. And a blanket to wrap the baby in, and diapers." The doc frowned then. "And a crib. You do have those things, don't you? I know you're stuck out here, but you should have been planning for the inevitable."

Doc was right. He'd had plenty of time to arrange for Earl to get supplies for the baby. Then he remembered the crib he'd taken up to the loft. "I have a crib," he said, knowing full well Mary-Ellen would want Violet to have it. "I'm not sure about the other things, but I'll check."

"Ah yes, Mary-Ellen was well prepared for her new arrival." He shook his head. "Such a tragedy, but she would be glad to see the crib put to good use. Jacob, too. Off you go then." He suddenly waved Brandon out of the sitting room as Violet screamed again.

His heart was heavy as Brandon climbed the steps to the loft. The crib was in perfect condition, as he knew it would be. It was the reason he hadn't made a crib himself. He searched about but couldn't find any diapers or baby clothes. They had to be there – he recalled Jacob talking about Mary-Ellen's delight at choosing clothing for the unborn baby.

He was confused – they had to be here somewhere. Then he remembered the spare room. That was destined to become the baby's room when it was older. Brandon hadn't gone into that room at all since they arrived. It had been only used for storage as far as he could tell and he hadn't disturbed any of the boxes. Now was the time to do that.

He carried the crib down from the loft and took it straight outside to air. I shouldn't be too dusty as he'd covered it the day he took it up there. He gave the bedding a good shake out anyway. Brandon then headed to that second bedroom. He felt like a thief in the night going through the bags and boxes in that room, but it was a fruitful exercise.

He found dozens of diapers, as well as baby clothes. Amongst the clothes were several knitted layettes, mostly yellow and green. Perfect for a baby not yet born. There were also small blankets perfect for swaddling a newborn.

Doc was right – Mary-Ellen was well prepared.

He snatched up a few diapers, a swaddling blanket, and one layette. When she was up to it, Violet would enjoy sorting through this lot, even if her heart was thinking of Mary-Ellen and Jacob's unborn baby.

As he hurried back to the Doc, he heard a long drawn-out scream and then a baby crying. His breath hitched in his throat. He was a father! He almost ran to the bedroom to be by his wife's side. Brandon was fully aware that under any other circumstances, he wouldn't be allowed in that room this early. He would be kept at arm's length until the doc had cleaned up and sorted out *the business end of things*, as doc preferred to call it.

Doc turned to face him as Brandon rushed into the room. "I found everything you need," Brandon said, then noticed the baby in the doc's hands. It was all he could do not to weep.

"Meet your son," Doc said. "Let's get this boy wrapped, to keep him warm." He lay the baby on the bed and deftly placed the diaper on him, then swaddled him and handed him over to his exhausted mother.

Tears rolled down her cheeks as she stared into her newborn son's face. "He's beautiful," Violet said, then reached for Brandon. He kneeled on the floor beside her.

"He certainly is, just like his mother," he said as he kissed her forehead.

"Have you thought of a name?" Doc asked as he packed up his medical equipment.

Violet thought for a moment, then glanced over at Brandon. "What do you think about Andrew? Without my brother, we would never have got together," she said wearily. "And I would never have fallen in love with you."

Did he hear correctly? "You… love me? You've never told me." More's the pity. Until this moment, Brandon thought it was all one-sided.

"Of course, silly. Did you think I would share a bed with someone I despised?"

"I love you more than life itself." He'd told her often enough before, but wanted to ensure she knew.

He should have known she loved him. His heart told him, but without the words, he had no confirmation.

"Your wife needs to rest now," Doc said, taking the baby from Violet and handing him to Brandon.

The new father leaned in and kissed her gently, then quietly left the room as she was already asleep. He would never forget this day as long as he lived.

Epilogue

Eight months later…

Brandon couldn't help but stare as Violet held their son, who was trying to climb down off her knee. He was crawling now, and Brandon was convinced it wouldn't be long before young Andrew would be walking. Then they really would have their work cut out for them.

Neither of them could bear to find out if Violet was still in danger. The life they'd made together, albeit on a ranch they didn't own, was idyllic, and they didn't want to leave. Not ever.

It meant they didn't leave the confines of the ranch, but that suited them both. Why would you leave heaven, especially if it put Violet in harm's way?

Andrew was a delightful baby and Brandon knew if his namesake was aware of his nephew's existence, provided it was safe to do so, he would adore the boy. It was his greatest regret, but Violet was living the life he believed she was destined for. The first time he met her, Brandon knew that life was not for her. Not really. She rallied against the restraints of her upper class life and seemed to want a far simpler life.

Now she had it, and was blissfully happy.

The one thing he regretted, was not being able to restore Jacob's ranch back to its full potential. Paddocks full of livestock, cowhands wandering about – that's what he remembered most about this place, along with the love between Jacob and Mary-Ellen. Without making themselves known to the townsfolk, there was no chance of the ranch getting back to what it once was.

The ruckus outside told Brandon they had visitors. These days it didn't cause the terror it once had, and although he still wore his gun-filled holster, he'd never needed to use it. Much to Violet's delight.

Glancing through the window, he could see Earl was one of their visitors, but who was the other man? He had his back to Brandon, and he couldn't make him out. Earl clutched a wad of papers. It got more and more curious by the minute.

He opened the door. "Earl! This is a pleasant surprise." The other man turned to face him, and his heart sank. He waved them both in.

"You don't seem pleased to see me," Andrew said, but his words were in mirth, not with animosity. More than anything, Brandon worried this was the end of their blissful lives here on the ranch. "You certainly know how to hide your existence – I've spent close to a year trying to find you both. I ended up hiring a detective agency." He sighed, then brightened up. "I have news," he said, gazing across the room toward his sister. His eyes then landed on their child. He turned to Brandon, his resentment clear in his expression. "I told you…"

"Not your choice," Brandon snapped.

"You forced me into marriage," Violet growled. "Anything after that, it was out of your hands." She stared at her brother until he shrugged his shoulders and his expression softened.

"You're both right. Of course you are. Who is this?" he asked, pointing toward their son and effectively changing the subject.

"This young man is your nephew. His name is Andrew." Brandon watched as Violet's brother swallowed back his emotion. He stepped over to the boy and picked him up. "Hello Andrew," he said. "I'm your uncle Andrew."

The baby's head shot up at the use of his name, and confusion clouded his face. One day he'd get it sorted, Brandon was certain. Andrew clutched the boy momentarily, then put him back on the floor. Then he walked over to his sister. As she stood, he appeared shocked. There was no hiding her over-sized baby bump. He hugged her tight, but made no comment.

"We came with good news," Earl finally announced once everyone was settled. "First, it's now safe for you to leave the ranch. The criminals who threatened to kill Violet are all behind bars." He opened the envelope he'd been clutching. The envelope that hadn't escaped Brandon's attention. "This next bit of news affects you, Buck."

Buck. No one had called him that for a very long time. "It's about the ranch." The news he'd feared since the day they arrived. They'd broken the law settling here, and now he had to pay the consequences. Brandon sat himself down and waited.

"Do you remember old Sherman Evans?"

Brandon was puzzled, but only momentarily. "The lawyer?"

"That's him. He died a few months after you left Angel's Bend."

"I'm sorry to hear that," Brandon said, and he was sorry. Sherman was a good man. "But what's that got to do with me?" Truthfully, he knew exactly what it had to do with him. He was about to to be told he was being hauled off to jail for living on someone else's property without permission.

"The town has been without a lawyer until only a few months back. Sherman's nephew has taken over his uncle's business, and has slowly been sorting through boxes of paperwork. They had all been stored when Sherman died."

Brandon wished Earl would get to the point. "What are you trying to say?" His heart thudded. After all this time, their happy days were over.

He rifled through the papers, then handed a small bundle to Brandon. "It's Jacob's will. Not that he expected to die when he did, but he had it all in hand."

And there it was. Despite Jacob telling Brandon he had no family, he did have. The ranch belonged to whoever that was. A complete stranger was going to take over the home he and Violet had made together.

He was totally stricken.

"Buck! Read it!" Earl demanded.

He did as he was told, then read it again, and once more for clarity.

"Brandon? You're scaring me," Violet said. "What does it say?"

He turned to her, confusion clouding his mind. "It says Jacob left his property and everything on it to me."

Violet hurried over to him and read Jacob's will for herself. "Does that mean…?"

"It means Buck is the legal owner of this ranch and all the property attached to it. It means," he continued, "you can stay here as long as you want."

Brandon's heart pounded. *How could that be true?* They were friends, he and Jacob, and Mary-Ellen too, but never would he have thought he would inherit their property. He'd always adored it, and had told Jacob how peaceful it was out here, but still… "I can't believe it. How can that be true?"

"It's been verified, and found to be completely legal."

Andrew interrupted then. "I was hoping Violet would come back home with me now that it's safe for her to do so." He appeared deflated.

Violet stiffened in Brandon's arms, and he stared down at her. He didn't want her to leave, he loved her far too much, but it was entirely her choice.

She leaned into him and his arm tightened around her. "I'm not going anywhere. I love it here, and I love Brandon." She glared at her brother then. "If you came to force me to go with you, forget it. Sheriff," she said, turning to Earl. "I refuse to go. If this man tries to make me, I want him arrested."

Brandon grinned. That's the Violet he loved, the one who stood up for herself. That said, he was very glad she didn't do that before they were married. Their lives would be a lot different now otherwise.

Earl looked confused and glanced from her brother across to Violet. "Mr. Southerby, do you intend to force your sister to leave with you? If so, I need to arrest you." The slightest smile tugged at his lips.

Andrew frowned. "Of course not! I can see how much in love they are. And frankly, if I had the choice, I'd live out here too."

Violet ran to her brother and hugged him. "Thank you," she said, her voice full of emotion. "The last thing I want to do is argue."

Andrew wrapped his arms around Violet and hugged her back. "Me either." He turned to Brandon then. "Since you know own this property, and I had no opportunity before this, I have a wedding gift for you."

Brandon studied him curiously. "We don't need gifts. We live a simple life."

"Don't argue. You need livestock. That is my wedding gift, and I expect you to accept." He turned to Earl. "Can you help me with that? And for goodness' sake, Brandon, get rid of that awful beard."

"Gladly. The darned thing itches." Everyone laughed and Brandon felt a weight lifted off his shoulders at everything that had occurred since their visitors arrived. His wife was safe, and they could live out their days here on the ranch they'd come to know as home.

He pulled Violet close and said a silent prayer of thanks. He also prayed for the souls of Jacob and Mary-Ellen and their unborn baby, as he had many times before. Without them, he would not have his own beautiful family and a life of peace and tranquility.

From the Author

Thank you so much for reading my book – I hope you enjoyed it.

I would greatly appreciate you leaving a review where you purchased, even if it is only a one-liner. It helps to have my books more visible!

About the Author

Multi-published, award-winning and bestselling author Cheryl Wright, former secretary, debt collector, account manager, writing coach, and shopping tour hostess, loves reading.

She writes both historical and contemporary western romance, as well as romantic suspense.

She lives in Melbourne, Australia, and is married with two adult children and has six grandchildren. When she's not writing, she can be found in her craft room making greeting cards.

Links

Website: *http://www.cheryl-wright.com/*

Facebook Reader Group:
https://www.facebook.com/groups/cherylwrightauthor/

Join My Newsletter:

https://cheryl-wright.com/newsletter/

www.ingramcontent.com/pod-product-compliance
Lightning Source LLC
Chambersburg PA
CBHW070622120726
47909CB00004B/1289

* 9 7 8 0 6 4 5 4 2 4 4 8 5 *